THE WAY

OF THE

SAINTS

Elizabeth Engelman

SOUTHEAST MISSOURI STATE UNIVERSITY PRESS | 2021

The Way of the Saints

Copyright 2021: Elizabeth Engelman

ISBN: 978-1-7330153-3-2
Softcover: $18.00

First published in 2021 by
Southeast Missouri State University Press
One University Plaza, MS 2650
Cape Girardeau, MO 63701
www.semopress.com

Disclaimer: *The Way of the Saints* is a work of fiction. The characters, events, and dialogue herein are fiction and are not intended to represent, refer to, nor disparage any known person or entity, living or dead.

Cover Design: Krystal Quiles

Library of Congress Cataloging in Publication Data
Engelman, Elizabeth, author.
The Way of the Saints / Elizabeth Engelman.
LCCN 2020052619 | ISBN 9781733015332 (paperback)
Classification: LCC PS3605.N4526 W39 2021 | DDC 813/.6--dc23
LC record available at https://lccn.loc.gov/2020052619

THE WAY

OF THE

SAINTS

Elizabeth Engelman

This book is for my mother and Grandmother

"Perhaps all the dragons in our lives are princesses who are only waiting to see us act, just once, with beauty and courage. Perhaps everything that frightens us is, in its deepest essence, something helpless that wants our love."

—Rainer Maria Rilke, *Letters to a Young Poet*

THE EYES OF NIGHT

EMPIRES ARE DEVILS DISGUISED AS GUARDIAN ANGELS.

—PEDRO ALBIZU CAMPOS

Puerto Rico
1923

"He eats with the dogs," said Rosendo's stepfather and doña Elba didn't object. She had no children of her own, and she would have paid more if not for the bruises and burn marks on Rosendo's skin. In the end, his stepfather felt satisfied he'd gotten a good price for the bastard—two forks, an iron kettle, a machete. He didn't care that the woman showed no interest in a son. She wanted nothing more than a vessel, a medium for her *espiritismo*.

For three years, Rosendo lived with the *espiritista* in her two-room hut, thick with the healing magic passed down from her ancestors. Elba divided the second room with a curtain and used it for her ceremonies. There she stored the instruments of her rituals—candles, rubbing alcohol, rum, oils, ginger, and coffee. Two burlap hammocks along with bundles of tobacco and herbs hung from the rafters above their heads like drying bridal bouquets. Rag dolls dressed as gypsies and warriors slumped against the walls, open-eyed and stitch-lipped.

Rosendo often awoke alone, confused by the soreness in his throat. Sometimes the muscles in his legs ached unexplainably as if he'd been running for many nights, bridled and mounted like a horse. He complained of tormenting voices. Said he needed rest.

Elba had told him to ignore the voices, and she gave him cane liquor to settle his nerves. Still, he felt the click of wings and tongues permeating his ears when he slept.

By eleven years old, Rosendo reached his limit and needed to learn the truth about Elba, about her healings. He squatted in the shrubs beneath doña Elba's hut. He hid, watching the ashen woman inside draw the shutters, and heard her bolt them with a latch. She was a mulatta, withered and bent like a knotted root, and as she hobbled back and forth across the stark room, he slipped his twig body into the crawl space and pressed his eye to a gap in the floorboards.

He couldn't make out her fragmented whispers, but he saw her prepare the healing ceremony in dim candlelight. Here at the edge of the mangrove swamp, the overhanging trees and thickets formed a canopy that blotted out the stars. Even on this clear evening, the small hut stood shrouded in pitch darkness.

His bare feet sank in the foul-smelling mud, and he strained his ears to hear her prayers begin. The voices inside were muffled below the shrill of insects and the call of the *coquí* frogs. If doña Elba caught him spying, she'd thrash him for sure.

On this particular night, Elba counseled with one of the *agregados*, a field hand who lived in the hacienda barracks. The villager wore a straw hat that shaded his leathery cheeks. Few men in the fields lived to their forties, but this man seemed older, stooped at the waist, deeply creased, and dragging a swollen foot wrapped in rags.

Elba arranged three wooden chairs in a sacred circle inside her hut. She sat in the wicker-backed chair, and the ragged man sat beside her. For a typical healing, Rosendo occupied the third chair. Tonight, though, for the first time in three years, he had feigned ill, and a small boy sat in his place. For fifteen cents and his best wooden knife, Rosendo had convinced the boy from the *barrio* to sit in the third chair. The boy's curiosity surprised him. He was eager to participate in the healing, and Rosendo realized he had bargained away his knife like a fool when the money would have satisfied the boy.

On the island, spiritists held minor celebrity status, and among the villagers, Elba had a cult following. Rosendo tried not to feel guilty. It wasn't like he'd forced the boy to take his place. It was a free choice, a generous trade. Later, Rosendo would wonder what had become of the child and feel regret, but for now, he pushed those feelings aside. He suspected Elba knew their time together was growing short. Recently, he'd begun crying out in his sleep, and on several occasions, he'd caught her frowning at his shaking hands. She made no fuss and asked no questions when Rosendo brought the boy to her, with his four missing front teeth, girlishly long lashes, and dimpled cheeks. To her, it made no difference, one child or another, as long as the paying client received a healing. She told Rosendo to sleep in the mangrove forest and return at dawn. Instead, he hid under the hut and watched.

He studied Elba as she used coal to mark a wide circle around the chairs. She dipped her fingers into an higuera-bark bowl filled with holy water and sprinkled the water on the circle. She used oil from a vial to anoint the temples, nostrils, lips, and eyes of the villager. The toothless boy looked bone thin as he sat in the chair typically reserved for Rosendo. His eyes darted like a hen's, bulging and frightened, in the candlelight. His feet did not reach the floor.

Elba placed white candles on the northern and southern points of the circle, and beside each candle she placed shells filled with water and earth. Rosendo knew how to arrange the sacred objects. What he didn't know was how to heal the villagers. As soon as Elba began to pray, he would fall asleep only to awake the next morning with the client gone and no memory of the healing. The chairs sat empty and Elba's burlap hammock lay untied and bundled in a corner.

On this night, Rosendo watched the ceremony with dread for the boy weighing heavily on his chest. As Elba began to invoke the healing spirits, she spoke louder, and he could discern bits and pieces of the words. The boy squirmed in his seat. His legs shook and sweat beaded on his skin.

Gnats flapped to Rosendo's face. Several times he wiped them from the corners of his eyes, but as Elba's words grew clearer, his movements diminished. The hairs on his arms pricked. Stone still, he trapped his breath in his chest to keep from making a sound. Then he heard the woman pray, invoking the spirits to take human shape without deformity or horror.

Rosendo felt the atmosphere around him change. The boy's head dropped limp at the shoulders. Rosendo's own body goosefleshed in response to the familiar words of the prayer. A hypnotic, uncontrollable quivering passed over him as he felt the rush of energy in the room pull at his raw edges. He felt light-headed, like he could drift up through the floor, pass through the room, over the hut, over the village, and then beyond.

Elba said, "Almighty Lord, who sees this man's miseries, permit the heavenly beings to come forth and make answers to my questions, fulfill my requests."

Rosendo dug his fingernails into his own arm to resist the pull, to stay awake, to stay grounded.

The boy jerked. His chin lifted up from his chest, and his eyes sprang open, unfocused. From his mouth a thunderous voice erupted. "Give me the child."

"Agreed," said Elba. "Body and soul."

The boy slipped off his chair and lurched onto the ground. Elba paid him no mind. Instead, she moved toward the villager to examine his leg. She removed the stained cloth and left the reeking rags in a pile while she retrieved a basin to wash the leg. She and the villager whispered and nodded to one another, looking pleased. They ignored the boy, who was now thrashing in abandon. He lay on the ground whimpering. His rigid limbs convulsed. From his hiding place, Rosendo watched, and his own body trembled. He knew he had betrayed the boy. He'd given him the money and the wooden knife knowing it wasn't safe. Yet he'd convinced the boy to be the dog of spirits.

Now, Rosendo had no doubt. Elba swapped in flesh and energy. She was a slave trader with the dead.

As vegetable bats swarmed above the shack's corrugated tin roof, Rosendo silently squirmed out from the crawl space and ran. His frantic course led him past the thatch-covered latrine, stumbling down the muddy ravine, wading through thickets of mangroves. Low branches scratched at him, and a labyrinth of roots jutted up from mud and shallow water. He clutched overhanging branches for support, banging his legs on the arched roots. When he broke through the thickets, he plunged into the chest-high water of the ravine and waded for three quarters of a mile to the mouth of the lagoon.

Elba kept her fishing canoe tied to a towering Ceiba tree close to the shore. Rosendo didn't dare take it. Even if he wanted to, it was too dark to waste time searching. He knew she would track him in the daylight, but by water there would be no sign of him, no steps to trace in the thick mud. Without the canoe, perhaps she would think him dead, having drowned in the lagoon. He was a good swimmer. He would take his chances with the water snakes, though he'd make sure to stay in shallow waters where he could touch bottom. When he needed to rest, he could take cover under the canopy of the mangroves. He could swim down shore, find the road. He had no plan other than to find the road. From there, he could at least escape the village.

As Rosendo swam, he fought back grotesque images of the boy convulsing in pain. He wondered if the boy's mother lay awake that night, anxious for her missing son. Would she search for him? Come morning, would Elba send him home?

Rosendo remembered the last time he had seen his own mother. She had been washing clothes in the river. Tied to her back was his toddler brother. Her bare arms glistened in the sunlight as they dipped in and out of the water. Why hadn't his own mother searched for him? Had she replaced him with her new son? Forgotten him?

Rosendo paddled harder, trying to put more distance between his thoughts and the shack he was leaving behind. Then he heard the faint sound of his name called through the swamp. *Rosendo*, it called in the voice of his mother. The name carried over the water. *Rosendo* he heard again. It was a feather-light sound, a dirty trick of the spirits. *Rosendo*, he heard for a third time.

Elba said three was the number for destiny. Rosendo swam deeper, too terrified to look back.

DEDICATION

Lower East Side, Manhattan
1974

The air smelled of piss and winos. Isabel stood in the dimly lit hall of Ernesto's building and held her breath. Overhead, a dying light flickered. Her mother, who owned only one book, the Bible, and devoted an hour to reading from it each morning, would be furious to discover Isabel pocketing Ernesto's address and now standing at his metal door. In the old neighborhood, he was known as *El Diablo.*

From a neighboring apartment, she heard sharp voices, then the racket of a baby crying, a radio blasting rhythmic salsa. She needed to get out of the hall. Halls weren't safe. She pounded on Ernesto's door with her fist.

A shadow slid across the peephole, and the deadbolt clicked. With the brass chain still latched, the door opened two inches, and Isabel saw one gray eye.

"Ernesto, it's Isabel. We spoke on the phone."

Without answering, the face withdrew and the door slammed shut. She heard the chain fall loose before it opened again. Ernesto stood in the doorway haggard, older than she remembered. One eye was clouded with a cataract, reminding her of moonstone.

"Isabel! All grown." He waved her into the apartment.

"Blanca," he shouted into the next room. "Look who's here. Little Isabel from the old building." As they walked into the living room, Isabel smelled rubbing alcohol, tobacco, and clove.

9

The smell bled out from the kitchen, and it surprised her that she hadn't noticed it from the hall. Papers and books were stacked in sloppy piles on the floor. Food-stained plates and glasses littered the coffee table. Cowrie shells, white candles, frosted jars, seed bead necklaces, a bottle of rum, and an ash tray with the bud of a cigar all lay on a larger wooden table near the kitchen. Then Isabel noticed Ernesto's wife, Blanca, sitting upright on the couch, completely asleep with a plate of chicken legs on her lap.

"Never mind that," Ernesto said with a nod at his wife. "Come, we'll work in the bathroom."

She hadn't known what to expect, but being confined with Ernesto in the bathroom was not what she'd imagined.

Her older brother Esau rarely spoke of Vietnam, but once, he'd sent a letter where he described a night on ambush patrol—how he hid in the jungle waiting for the enemy when a tiger stalked right by him, looked at him from the corner of its eye. Tigers went after the guys who fell asleep, attacking at least one sleeping soldier a month. *You don't turn your back on a tiger*, he wrote.

Isabel followed Ernesto through the apartment. She was rigid, on alert. The farther she walked down the musty hall, the more she felt her gut twisting. She regretted coming already, but she'd given up on her last doctor. She needed help, and turning to Ernesto was a risk she was willing to take. She'd do whatever he said.

The morning paper reported the chilliest Memorial Day in years, but it was warm in the apartment. Still, she didn't take off her thin coat. Ernesto stepped aside in the narrow hall and gestured for her to enter the bathroom. She squeezed by him, not wanting to touch his chest. The room, with its wall-to-wall peach tile, was no wider than a bath mat. It looked recently cleaned and smelled of pine. She stood in the cramped space between the toilet and the bathtub feeling idiotic, fragile. She shivered and struggled to breathe. It was too stuffy, too warm. Sour.

"You know," she stammered. "I think I've made a mistake."

"It's fine, *todo está bien, mija*." His soothing, paternal tone rankled her further. He still possessed the kind of beast presence she remembered from her girlhood.

"I can help you," he said.

"I want this baby," she said, laying a hand on her flat stomach. "It's just." She didn't have the words to express her dread, the hopeless look on her doctor's face. "They said I couldn't. I mean, I've tried, but . . ." She looked down at her feet.

"Nothing's impossible." Ernesto reached out a palm towards Isabel and squeezed her shoulder.

Startled by his touch, she took a step back.

"I won't hurt you." He stepped closer, and she noticed his long fingernails and the silver, serpentine ring around his index finger.

"Do you mind?" He cleared his throat and helped her slip her arms out of her jacket.

She studied a yellowed crack in the ceiling, anything to avoid direct eye contact. "Getting pregnant isn't the problem," she said to the crumbling drywall. "I lost the others." Her face flushed.

"I understand," he said. He leaned over the white porcelain tub and began filling a shallow plastic basin with warm water. Over the sound of the running water he said, "You're not the first to come here from the old building. What's it been, twelve years?" He laid the basin at her feet.

"Fourteen."

"Take off your shoes." He gestured to the basin with his chin. "Get in."

Isabel slipped out of her platform shoes and placed her red beret on the closed toilet lid. Before stepping into the basin, she rolled her wide-leg jeans into large cuffs right below the knee. A wave of warmth crept up her calves as the liquid rose to her ankles.

"Better remove your blouse, too," he said. "Don't want to ruin your pretty clothes." His expression was blank. Matter of fact, like a doctor's, but she felt the muscles in her shoulders tense up and she clenched her fists into tight knots.

She sized up the old man's lean body. She could kick his ass. She'd beaten men before. Kicked José Martínez in the balls after he'd cheated and mouthed off, busted Carlos Moreno's nose for getting fresh with her in a dark stairwell, almost shoved the fifth-floor junkie Manuel down the elevator shaft when he went for her purse. The *pendejo* Manuel got away, but she'd give Ernesto hell if she had to. She took a deep breath and decided with a nod. She could scream, wake up his wife. She broadened her narrow shoulders and straightened her back.

She pulled her blouse over her head, frizzing her hair, and immediately wrapped her arms around her bra and chest.

Ernesto draped a dank, pink towel over her bare shoulders.

From a medicine cabinet above the sink, he pulled out a bottle of rubbing alcohol. He poured a splash of the alcohol into his cupped palm and rubbed both hands together. Then, with dripping fingers, he smeared his palms into her hair, pressing it flat against her scalp. The feel of his stained hands with their long fingernails brushing against her skin made her stomach tighten. Stray drops of alcohol dripped down the back of her neck.

Her eyes burned from the smell, but she was afraid to close them. Ernesto mumbled rhythmic incantations in a language she didn't understand, and his body swayed. He waved his hands in overlapping orbits above her head, down her back, in front of her stomach, and between her thighs. Then, from an ashtray balanced on the rim of the tub, Ernesto lit a slender cigar and blew smoke first into her left ear and then her right. With quick exhales, he blew smoke into her face until she choked and coughed. He blew smoke down the front and back of her body. She stood engulfed in a cloud of smoke as the walls in the bathroom drew closer. Blinded by the smoke and the stinging smell, the lines of Ernesto's face slipped in and out of focus, until he no longer looked like a man, but more like an empty-eyed skull. Smoke filled her lungs, burned her throat. Her body weakened. The room spun. There was the sensation of falling. Hitting the ground. Slapping tile before slipping right through the floor. Sinking without end.

Isabel couldn't tell how long she'd been standing there with rubbing alcohol in her hair and cigar smoke trapped in her lungs, but when Ernesto completed the cleansing, the water in the basin licked ice cold against her legs and pruned soles of her feet.

"You've done very well," Ernesto said. "Get dressed and we'll discuss your case in the kitchen."

They passed Ernesto's wife, who still sat on the couch with its plastic cover and faded floral design, the plate of chicken reduced to bones on her thighs. With her head cocked back and her lips parted, gentle snores slipped from the woman's throat. Isabel had to remove several books from a wooden chair before she could sit down. A trickle of alcohol dripped down the back of her ear. With shaking hands, she wiped it away.

Ernesto looked grave as he spoke hushed words just above a whisper. Isabel had to lean forward to hear.

"You're in danger," he said. "You're cursed."

On the opposite wall from where she sat, a bookshelf housed a collection of statues. Isabel shivered as she studied them. She recognized St. Anthony, Our Lady of Mercy, St. Barbara, and St. Claire, standing erect as soldiers. The chalky whites of their eyes glared into the apartment, watching. One of the statues was unfamiliar. The carved wooden warrior held a fiery red sword in his fist. At his feet stood a tiny castle, and on his head was a crown.

Ernesto lit candles and turned out the overhead lights. The table was covered in white linen. He put a piece of chalk in one of Isabel's hands and a shiny black stone in the other.

"First, we must ask permission to do our work. Let us pray."

Ernesto prayed in an unintelligible language, while Isabel closed her eyes and listened. She ignored the voice in her head, her mother's chiding rebuke. Under no circumstances would she end up like her mother.

"Now that you're cleansed and we have permission, we can start the reading," he said. Ernesto rubbed the cowrie shells in his hands and tossed them onto the table like dice. "*Los caracoles*," he said. "The mouthpieces of the gods."

Several times, he asked Isabel to hold objects in her hands as he shook the toothy shells in his fist and dropped them. Then he studied how the shells scattered on the white tablecloth.

"This is an ancient language of divination," he said. "Older than the Egyptians. The Romans threw knucklebones. Called them *Tali*. Heel bones were thrown, too, called lots."

That sounded familiar. "You mean, like the soldiers throwing lots at the crucifixion?"

"For the robe of Christ? No. This, my dear, is not a game of chance. It's a language. You know your Bible?"

"A little. My papi was a Pentecostal preacher."

"No shit?" Ernesto nodded to himself. "I remember Rosendo well. Didn't take him for a religious man."

"He wasn't. But a lot of things changed after the old building burned down."

"That rathole was a firetrap. Must've been a hundred years old."

"We lost everything."

"Where's your family stay now?"

"They're still on Pitt Street."

"Good old Pitt." He dragged each word out in a singsong voice. "Don't miss it a bit. Stank like shit." He smiled with large yellow teeth and scratched his prickled chin.

Pitt Street, a seven-block stretch of crumbling walk-ups, ran from Henry Street to Houston. Nuyoricans called it *Loisada*, but the map read Lower East Side.

Her coat slipped to the ground and she repositioned it on the back of her chair. "Anyway, my mother's the real preacher in the family. She'd kill me if she knew—"

Ernesto tilted his head and grimaced. "You consulted with me?" His cloudy eye, shadowed in the candlelight, was no longer visible. It made him look one-eyed, and reminded Isabel of a coconut scarecrow, split.

She nodded and lowered her voice. "My mother wouldn't understand."

"Rest easy, child. I'm a high priest, a *babalawo*, a father of secrets. Your skeletons are safe with me." Ernesto studied the *caracoles* strewn across white linen and read the pattern.

"The *Odu* is a sign," he said. "It tells me about your life, the path you've walked, and how you arrived on it."

"What's it say?"

"I see tremendous negativity. There is much pain." As Ernesto continued to read the patterns, his tone was compassionate, but in her head his words detonated a land mine of memory.

Isabel is an eight-year-old tiptoeing across the front room of her family's tenement apartment. On the floor, Angel and her twin brothers sleep on mattresses. Clothes drying on lines hang above their heads like damp stars. From the kitchen, there is the sound of her mother crying out in pain. There is the explosive snap of her father's belt.

Ernesto reached across the table and gave Isabel's hand a squeeze. She jerked away.

"Do you need a break?" he said.

She shook her head. "I'm fine. Keep going."

Ernesto closed his eyes and sucked in a deep breath before studying the *caracoles* again.

Isabel, the girl, stands in her slippers and a thin daisy nightgown in the one-hundred-year-old walk-up of her childhood. Too short to see out of the eyehole, she unlocks the door and cracks it open. She gauges the seven steps between her apartment's front door and the communal bathroom in the hall. She scans the closed doors of the other three flats. The dim incandescent light bulb flickers overhead as she bolts for the toilet. In her nightgown, she is a dark waif with coarse hair.

Her oldest brother, Angel, waits for moments like these to catch her alone in the bathroom, to pin her to a stack of tires behind the building. She tells no one, not her sisters, not her mother. But when her 2nd grade classmates at Public School 4 call her Buckwheat, she will rage against them with her tiny fists.

Ernesto cleared his throat before speaking again. "You need purification to expel bad spirits. And protective beads."

15

"What about the baby?"

Isabel thought back to the first miscarriage, the cutting pain flashing down her middle, the blood between her thighs, her cupped palm trying to hold it back, her hands covered in loss, only eight weeks.

Ernesto said, "During your reading of the *caracoles*, I saw an image of a frog, bloated and dead. The eyes of the frog were sewn shut, sealed by the spirits. If we don't act quickly, the frog will be in the grave."

Isabel imagined the bloated frog with its fabric-thin eyes stitched and sealed. "I don't understand."

"Your womb," he said. "Your womb is the frog."

Her second miscarriage had been in a public restroom. Oh, God. Not here, she'd prayed. She'd covered the filthy toilet seat with paper, squatted with trembling legs, felt her innards empty.

She looked directly into Ernesto's face. "Please, whatever it takes. I'll do anything."

The third time doubled her over in pain. No heartbeat, the doctor had said. Fever. Probably infection. They'd scraped her nine-week-old baby away.

Ernesto nodded and sucked in a deep breath. "I'll do my best. It's a powerful curse."

"Who's done this to me? Why would anyone?"

"Curses are tricky things. They can be picked up like a bad smell, but some curses are passed down from generation to generation. From our fathers. From our father's fathers. When sent by an enemy, they are cast out into the world like an arrow. Other times, a person has opened a ruinous door in the spirit world that must be sealed shut."

Isabel nodded but hardly processed his words. She put a protective hand over her stomach. "What do I have to do?"

Ernesto rummaged through a stack of papers, pulled out a used envelope, and wrote on the back. First, he wrote an address and below it, what looked like a grocery list. He then wrote *$50* and underlined it twice. "My fee." He handed it to Isabel.

"Buy everything on the list," he said. "Don't forget a thing." He pointed to the address at the top of the paper. "This is the *botanica* shop owned by one of my goddaughters, Lourdes. I'll tell her you're coming. She'll have all you need. Don't worry, you can trust her." The tip of the pencil tapped the underlined number. Ernesto's voice was urgent. "It'll take time, money, and inner strength."

"This baby's mine." She folded the paper and put it in her purse.

"Me and Lourdes been doing this a long time," he said, in an attempt to reassure her. "You'll be a mother soon enough, but we must work quickly. Powerful forces have already claimed the baby inside you."

Behind the buildings on Pitt Street, children jumped on discarded mattresses and scaled stacks of junk tires. Isabel heard their shouting through the groan of traffic and the chatter of men who rolled dice or set up wood tables for dominoes.

She peered down through her dark glasses at the sidewalk, careful, like a superstitious girl avoiding the cracks. She gripped her handbag around her stomach, reminding herself of the ladies white-knuckling designer purses on the Upper West Side.

The smell of fish and waste off the East River made her queasy. She crossed the street and stepped into the shade of Our Lady of Sorrows Catholic Church. From her family's fourth-floor apartment, Isabel had a direct view of Our Lady of Sorrows. She could see the blood-red church with its white trim, arches, the massive circular window above the double doors, and the angular peaks crowned with wiry crosses.

The door to the botanica read, *Doing Business Since 1958*. It chimed with clinking brass bells when she opened it. Isabel paused in the doorway where she stood beside a three-foot-tall statue of Saint Barbara. The statue held a silver sword, and a dish of pennies rested at its bare feet. The store smelled of spices, and the air was a collision of earthy herbs and tangy incense. There were several short aisles, each lined with shelves. Isabel scanned them, not knowing where to start.

Handwritten labels in English and Spanish categorized the shelves into neat sections: Money, Love, Protection, Fast Luck, Jinx Removal, Health, Spell Breaking, Job Finding, Gambling, and Win in Court. Ritual candles were piled high on one shelf. Herbs were vacuum-sealed in clear plastic.

Against one wall, a large selection of candles in all sizes sat in colorful glass cylinders. Iconic images of saints decorated the fourteen-day prayer candles. Among the familiar saints were ones she didn't recognize. *Changó Macho* read one; *Ogun* read another. Below these were thin-pillared Hoodoo candles: Fast Cash Hoo Doo, Come To Me Hoo Doo, and Sucks to be You Mojo.

A woman in a long white skirt walked through a beaded curtain and acknowledged Isabel with a gentle smile. Her face was free of wrinkles despite her coarse gray hair, and in her arms, she held a cardboard box of skulls.

She placed the box of skulls on a glass counter and greeted Isabel. "*Buenos días,*" she said, "How can I help you?"

Isabel felt struck by the graceful way the woman clasped her long fingers and rocked back and forth on her heels. Everything about her seemed fluid, in motion.

"Hi," she said, "Ernesto sent me. He said I should ask for Lourdes."

The woman let out a little gasp, and her eyes gleamed with warmth and delight that put Isabel at ease. "At your service. You're the woman Ernesto told me about, sí?"

"Yes, I'm Isabel."

"*Mucho gusto.* I'm Lourdes. You're right on time."

Isabel looked around the cluttered shop. It was itching with breath and eyes, though it was completely empty apart from herself and the shop owner. "Then you know why I'm here?"

"Ernesto told me all I need to know. Don't worry about nothing."

*

Lourdes radiated empathy and confidence, and a wave of comfort swept over Isabel for the first time in weeks. It was like the woman saw below the surface and unmasked the hidden parts of her. Isabel took a deep breath and gripped the yellow notebook paper. "He gave me this list. Said I could find everything I needed here."

"That's right. No two ways about it." Lourdes gestured to the shelves with a flick of her bangled wrist. "I got the biggest shop in the whole city. Ernesto sends all his clients my way."

"You work together?"

"Over twenty years," said Lourdes. "He's my godfather."

"What, like Marlon Brando?"

"*¿Quién? ¡No, muchacha!* You're a funny lady." The woman patted Isabel on the shoulder, then held out her palm, the color of shined copper. "Let's see the list," she said, wiggling her fingers.

Isabel handed over the yellow paper. Lourdes plucked reading glasses from her nest of hair and adjusted them on her slim nose, magnifying light-brown eyes behind the glass. Her fingers glided down the page, and she pursed her lips as she read.

"It seems like a lot," Isabel said to break the silence.

"This," said Lourdes, unimpressed, "is no biggie. *Por favor, mija,* don't look so glum. We'll fix you. Everything we fix. Ernesto will finish what he started. And together, we won't leave a single door open. *Pero,* if you need special readings or services in the future, you come straight to me."

"You sure he won't mind?"

"No, *es la idea de Ernesto.* It's his professional recommendation. He told me so himself."

Isabel nodded again.

"Follow me," said Lourdes, and Isabel followed the woman down the aisles.

"I have the best quality shop in five boroughs," Lourdes said with pride. "I cater to everything. You want to make it rain money, *aquí*, right here, I got spells and kits galore." Lourdes gestured toward a shelf marked *Money-Dinero*, and Isabel examined its soaps, candles, and bottles of cologne. One plastic bottle had an inked image of a mustached man wearing a tuxedo and bow tie. It was labeled *Don Dinero* and held a forest-green liquid.

Lourdes pointed to the left and said, "Here's everything you need for love. Ah, this is what I want." She stopped in front of the shelf labeled *Jinx Removal-Corta Fluida*. From the shelf, she lifted a tall white candle with blue and white decorative crosses housed in a glass canister. "Takes away roadblocks," she said. "Uncrosses any situation." She lifted the candle and held it close to Isabel's face for her to inspect. "You like it?"

Isabel smiled, not knowing how to inspect a candle, and nodded in approval.

"I melt the wax myself. Then I add special oils." Lourdes winked at Isabel. "This helps ignite wishes. Don't look so worried. You'll see." She tucked the candle under her arm and used her index finger to scan the soaps. "We'll be wanting a bar of this." She grabbed a block of soap wrapped in red paper. Its logo was a devil and a black crow, and the label read, *Go Away Evil Soap*. "To command desires," she explained.

The afternoon was a haze of shopping for oils in tiny, brown vials, talismans, beaded necklaces, candles, and herbs. Beside the register was a carved replica of the Archangel Michael with gold wings and gold arrows. Beside the angels, Our Lady of Fátima statues and crucifixes sat in an assortment of sizes. Lourdes placed all of Isabel's items in a large paper grocery bag, adding up the cost with a calculator as she went. From the counter, she picked up a resin miniature Jesus. "That's on the house." She tossed Jesus into the large paper grocery bag. "Now, that'll be *$126.72. ¿Dólares o cheque?*"

Isabel's eyes widened. "That's more than I expected."

"Spells don't come cheap."

Ernesto should have warned her about the cost. After buying the items, she wouldn't have enough left for the taxi and would have to take the subway hefting a large grocery bag for several blocks. Irritated, she reached into her wallet and started counting the bills, thinking it would be rice and beans for a month if she weren't careful.

"*Para las gallinas,* you'll need to go to the live poultry market."

Isabel made a sour expression. "You mean a slaughterhouse?"

"The fresher the better."

"What's the hen for?"

"*Para* sacrifice," Lourdes said. "You will need blood."

Isabel smelled the live poultry market from under the Williamsburg Bridge before she saw it. It was early morning, her favorite time in the city, when the streets barely felt awake. She gave herself enough time to drop off the botanica bag with Ernesto, then ran back down stairs for her last errand. The Yellow Pages listed only a handful of live markets, but she was familiar with the kosher slaughterhouse close to Ernesto's apartment on Delancey.

Customers stood on feather-littered cement floors, patiently waiting in lines for the butchers. Others prodded squawking chickens in search of lively birds. Cage upon cage was stacked along one wall, creating a massive tower of chickens, and inside the cages squawked more fowl than Isabel had ever seen in her life. Fattened chickens were squashed three and four to a cage, and the whole store reverberated with the sound of panicked chirps and the distressed rustle of feathers flapping against metal.

A butcher wearing an apron flecked with chicken flesh worked beside a trashcan brimming with intestines. His blood-spattered rubber boots came to his knees, and his cap sat low over his eyes as he spoke in broken Spanish to a woman inquiring about the daily price of chicken feet.

"Give me the whole chicken," Isabel heard the woman say. The butcher opened a cage and pulled out a honey-colored chicken by its legs. In a fit, the upside down chicken spread its wings and thrashed. It seemed to put up quite a fight until the man knotted a cord around its legs and suspended it from a scale. Then it fell still, stunned and silent.

"Five pounds," said the butcher. He walked over to a nearby table and tapped at a calculator. "You want it cut up?"

"Four pieces," the woman said. He scribbled something down on a pad, ripped off a square of paper, and handed it to the woman. "Take this to the window," he said, handing her the pay slip. "It'll be about ten minutes." Then he untied the bird and walked it behind a clear plastic curtain, which divided the front of the store with the back slaughter room.

Isabel stood in line behind the woman. She heard the *kuh-kuh-kuh-KACK!* of a rooster, an air raid siren that made her want to drop to the sawdust to take cover. When it was her turn, she had to shout her order over the sound of sharpening knives and the chatter of caged birds.

"I'll need a hen," she said.

"Sure thing," said the worker. "Plucked and cleaned?"

"No. I need this one alive, please."

The man pulled a silver and white-flecked hen from a cage. His large, swift hands tied its feet with a cord and weighed the bird upside down just as she had seen before. All the while, he kept his gaze locked on Isabel. "Those eyes," he said to himself but loud enough for her to hear. Only it sounded more like *doze eyes*, and she smiled. He wasn't her type, too thin, too short, but she appreciated a flirt and felt energized by the boost of confidence. "We got a sale on duck, too," he said. "I'll give you a good deal."

"No, thanks. Just the guinea hen."

"Whatever you say, boss." The man shrugged and disappeared behind the large plastic curtain. Within minutes, he returned with a canvas sac. He unknotted the hen from the scale, but refastened the feet before placing the hen in the bag and then into a cardboard box.

"From coop to soup." The man laughed and handed her a slip of paper and the twitching box. "You pay at the counter. Come back and see me real soon, beautiful."

With one arm, she positioned the box under her armpit. "Thanks," she said, and as she turned to walk away, she overheard the woman behind her ask for lamb on the bone.

Isabel balanced her purse on her shoulder and the box on her opposite hip. The hen was as light as a small dumbbell, but it unnerved her to feel it rustle inside the bag. She was weighed down on all sides and was thankful Ernesto lived only a few blocks from the market.

Ernesto made a mixture of the dry herbs and oils from the botanica combined with Isabel's urine. He poured the liquid into a plastic bottle and instructed her to shake it multiple times.

She felt repulsed but determined. A healthy pregnancy was her ticket out of her house and out of the city.

Next, he wrote tiny words on a small scroll, and, with black electrical tape, he secured the folded scroll to her right shoe. "To step on your enemies," he said. With other items from her grocery bag, he prepared a lotion to rub on her belly and gave her a golden amulet to pin to her bra.

This time, with his wife Blanca's help, they covered the wooden table with the same white linen from the day before. On the cloth, they placed sixteen small cowrie shells. Beside the shells, he placed other objects from the grocery bag, lit the candles, and shut off the lights.

Blanca was told to sit at the north end of the table, while Ernesto sat to the south. Isabel sat between them.

"Together, we will read the shells to see which saint will protect you and your daughter," he said.

Isabel sat up at this. "It's a girl? I'm having a girl?"

"I saw her in a dream."

"Get on with it," said Blanca. "We haven't much time."

"She's right," he said. "There's a battle for the baby. Let's begin."

Ernesto prayed for several minutes in a strange language. Isabel lowered her head, closed her eyes, and prayed in her own heart. *Help my baby. Help my baby.*

Ernesto's voice rose as he prayed, and fear glued Isabel's eyes shut for several minutes. The atmosphere in the kitchen shifted, thick and cold. Blanca quivered in her seat, so much so that Isabel peeked at her. In the candlelight, her dilated pupils were two black moons. Then Blanca's mouth fell open, and she spoke, her voice deep, cracked, and alien.

"How dare you summon me to this place," said the voice. "I have a job. You must not stand in my way."

"How dare you speak to me like that," said Ernesto. His voice rose above his wife's. He stood, knocking over his chair in the process.

Terror filled Isabel. Ernesto glared at his wife, and Isabel recoiled, thinking he might slap Blanca. She wanted to run, but her fear gripped her to her chair.

Blanca meekly replied, "Oh, master, I didn't know it was you. I didn't see you."

"Silence. Who are you?" said Ernesto.

"I am the keeper of the babies."

"You have no right," he said. "I command you to leave at once."

"But you can't get us all."

"And why the hell not?"

A sinister smile braided across Blanca's features. "We are many."

Ernesto placed a fishbowl full of water in front of Blanca. He made a cupping motion over her head and dropped something invisible into the bowl. Isabel saw nothing in his hands, but the water made a plunk and stirred.

Isabel had been raised to believe in unseen powers. Hadn't women filled with the Holy Spirit in her father's church spoken in undecipherable tongues? Hadn't deacons driven out demons in the name of Jesus? How could this be wrong if Ernesto was using his powers to save her baby? Would a devil cast out devils? Isabel had set her heart on a baby, an end to her miserable loneliness, someone to truly love her. Was this the only way?

"The dark spirits are dissolved in water," Ernesto said. Twenty-six times, voices came from Blanca's mouth, snarling, cursing, and gurgling voices. Each time, Ernesto commanded them to depart and dropped the invisible forces into the water.

Ernesto fisted the cowrie shells and shook his hand over the table. "We need to act fast." He tossed the shells onto the table, examined the pattern, and said the name. "*Yemayá*, mother of all, what do you want in exchange for protecting this woman and her baby?" With each new toss, he scribbled a new list of ingredients on his yellow pad of paper. More chicken, more herbs, more powders, and candles.

Isabel's heart sank. Not again. This was costing her a small fortune, and after her last visit to the slaughterhouse, she had no money left.

Even if she worked overtime, she wouldn't earn enough to buy all the additional items he had listed. She would have to borrow the money from her family. She'd have to lie. Her mind raced, spinning a convincing story for Rosa, the most compassionate of her older sisters. A stolen wallet, a mugger on the subway. Or maybe better to say she lost the wallet, dropped it accidentally down a gutter.

"We'll need it all to prepare for battle," Ernesto said.

"You need more?" she said. "I thought . . ."

"Niña, these things are very delicate. Where's your respect?"

"I'm sorry," she said, feeling reprimanded. "I understand."

Ernesto flicked on the overhead lights, and they agreed to meet the next morning at nine to complete the ceremony.

"One last thing," he said. "Did you bring the picture?"

Isabel reached into her purse and pulled out the Polaroid of Jude.

In the picture, he rested one hand on the leather seat of his Triumph motorcycle. His other hand, he'd shoved deep into his jeans pocket. Jude kept his hands to himself. It was one of the qualities Isabel liked most about him. He didn't grope or paw. That, and his way of making self-deprecating jokes with a wicked smile.

On their first date, he had taken Isabel to a Chinese buffet. All you can eat. "Stuff yourself," he said, and then went about the serious business of eating three full plates of shrimp lo mein, moo goo gai pan, and egg foo young. It was then, sitting across from him in that booth, that she noticed everything about Jude seemed specked with paint, spotted with oil stains. From the canvas boat shoes, to the leather motorcycle vest, to the anchor medallion around his thick neck. All of it was tainted somehow, greased. A sliver of cracked cement even clung to the blonde hair on his muscular forearm. He didn't try to impress her, and somehow the not trying seemed impressive. A man who didn't give a rat's ass set himself apart in her mind as refreshing. She found his confidence attractive. His courtesy, attentive. His passiveness, safe. She figured the untidy bits about him were all things she could change. Malleable potential she could press and hammer.

Jude lived at the seventy-ninth Street Boat Basin on his fifty-seven-foot Chris-Craft Catalina, a yacht he bought off the bandleader Guy Lombardo. *The Lady Viking* was a beauty, with twin diesel engines, a fiberglass deck, and radiators in every room. He was what they called a live-aboard, staying in the master cabin year-round.

Rent was dirt cheap compared to the apartments on the neighboring Upper West Side. Retirees on fixed incomes, writers, artists, and men like Jude all called the marina their permanent residence. They were pioneers who preferred the serpentine hiss of a winter swell than the drug-infested walk-ups of the city. Instead of cul-de-sacs, they had mooring fields.

When the weather was good, Jude invited Isabel to join him on *The Lady Viking* around Manhattan Island. They sliced up the Hudson River in the face of a breakneck wind all the way to the Tappan Zee Bridge.

She imagined a life out of Pitt Street and tethered to the docks on the banks of the Hudson River. She envisioned her morning coffee on deck watching the idyllic horizon. She liked the idea of seagulls passing overhead and fish jumping below. Where else could a person see the full arc of the moon yet still be in Manhattan?

She bought *The Joy of Sex* and *The Joy of Cooking* in that order.

What Jude lacked in motivation, she made up for in tenacity.

*

E rnesto held the Polaroid of Jude in his stained hands. "Are you absolutely sure this is the baby's father?"

"I'm sure."

Ernesto pinched the photo between his fingers. Then, with a surgeon's precision, he pierced Jude's pale, blue eyes with a sharp pin.

LA TORMENTA

Fajardo, Puerto Rico
1937

A group of teenage girls swayed in the heat to the strumming of the conquistadores' guitars. One man scratched a *guillo*, a hollow gourd notched with ridges, while another pounded a traditional tambour drum. The air smelled of smoked pigs roasting in nearby pits.

While the other girls tried to catch the attention of the musicians, Paula scanned the faces in the crowd, disappointed. She wished Alberto hadn't gone off to Ponce with the other *Independentistas* to protest the arrest of Pedro Albizu Campos. She watched with half-interest as men and women from the village strolled with their ceremonial palm branches down Calle Principal. With clasped hands behind her back, she imagined Alberto, handsome in his black and white Liberation Army uniform, marching down the city center in the southern town. She imagined the stomp of boots and the jeers of spectators and wished she could have joined him.

The Party had organized trucks for Nationalists from as far as the western town of Mayaguez to march in the Ponce parade, but when the trucks pulled into Fajardo, Paula didn't dare ask her brother Maximo if she could go. She knew he would never permit it. Still, she envied the young girls in the Nurses Corp boarding the trucks alongside the cadets in their smart, white uniforms. She remembered one of the spirited girls waving and shouting, "¡*Viva*

29

Puerto Rico Libre!" as the truck pulled away. Alberto had smiled at the girl, and Paula wished she hadn't noticed the admiration in his eyes. She felt plain, invisible in comparison. Left behind.

His absence spoiled the smaller Palm Sunday gathering in Fajardo. Paula glanced over the heads of the crowd, and was considering walking home when she noticed Rosendo, Alberto's older brother, leaning against an iron lamppost, his brazen eyes locked on her. He stood a head taller than the other men and spoke with an elderly peasant who sat on a cement bench rolling tobacco paper between brown, stained fingers. As he spoke, his eyes remained on Paula.

Minutes later, he was beside her, tipping his fedora to the group of girls. He wore his collar open, exposing a hairline crease of dirt around the base of his neck. His slacks and buttoned-down shirt, however, were unwrinkled and neat.

Several girls peeked back at him with admiring glimpses that he ignored.

He moved closer to Paula and shouted a greeting over the music before kissing her cheek. His breath smelled of rum, and his voice had a scratch like the *guillo.* He towered over her, handsome, with skin and hair as fair as a Yankee. His angular jaw recalled her history lessons of the Spaniards who walked the plaza four decades earlier in their starched suits and white shoes. Rosendo's clothes were plain and worn thin, but he had the straight posture of a gentleman and the smooth, confident demeanor of a gamecock.

"Look at you, all grown up," he said.

"It's good to see you again." Paula smiled politely, but her attention was diverted by the musicians.

"I haven't seen you in years. I hardly recognized you." With a sweep of his eyes, he took in the hem of her petal-shaped skirt, her narrow waist, the flame-orange blouse that exposed her collarbone. She felt like an ornamental tree, a spectacle, and blushed under his unabashed scrutiny.

"I had to get closer to know for sure, but I knew it, Paula. I knew it was you." He said her name as if he had some kind of claim on it. As if it were the most natural word on his lips.

She placed her hand on her brow to block the sun, creased her forehead, and squinted. "I thought you left," she said. "Didn't you take off to find work?"

"Yeah, but I'm back now." He pressed his lips into a line. "I'm sorry to hear about your parents. Alberto told me what happened. My condolences."

"Thank you," she said, her voice a whisper. She tried not to think of the year she'd turned fifteen, the year her parents had died only months apart from tuberculosis. To remember her family as it was, healthy and whole, only pained her now.

"I hear you stay with your brother," he said.

"You know Maximo?"

Rosendo shook his head. "Never spoken with him, but I've seen him selling his work pants at the hacienda commissary from time to time."

Her brother Maximo owned no land, and he rented the frame house where she lived on the outskirts of the village. His wife, Luz Marí, sewed denim slacks for field hands, and he traveled weeks at a time by foot, stagecoach, or electric bus, selling her handiwork from town to town. His business was small, but it afforded him what he needed: board walls, a galvanized roof, shoes on his children's feet, milled rice, and the occasional codfish.

"So, you work at one of the haciendas?" she said. She moved to put a respectable distance between them.

"Not anymore. I'm at the mill. But people around here know my brother, and your name's come up from time to time."

Paula smirked. "I didn't realize the men were such gossips."

"Worse than old women." Rosendo grinned, his eyes brightening. "Don't worry. Not an unkind word was ever said about you. Not yet."

"It's a small town," she said. "People talk."

"I'm not interested in gossip," he said.

She shifted her feet and wiped sweat from the back of her neck with her palm. "That's good. I'm afraid the gossip about me would bore you to tears."

31

"Don't tell me you don't have any juicy secrets from your schoolgirl days?"

Her formal schooling had ended with the death of her parents. Afterward, she had moved into her brother Maximo's frame home to help care for her nieces and nephews. In the two years since, she had remained cloistered in his house at the top of the ridge. With her brother often traveling for work, she lived a quiet life helping her sister-in-law. Entire days were devoted to scrubbing laundry by the banks of the river, her skirt pulled up to her thighs, squatting barefoot, laying clothes on the rocks to dry in the unbearable sun. Outings were rare, privacy impossible, and most months, her only social gatherings occurred on Saturday mornings when she celebrated the Sabbath at the *Iglesia Adventista*.

"Secrets?" she repeated nervously. "Unless you mean cleaning secrets, you're out of your mind." Despite her attempt to politely end their conversation, he ignored her cues.

"I suppose that sister-in-law of yours doesn't let you out of her sight," he said.

"I take care of her children." She didn't bother to add that in addition to her chores, her brother had procured work for Paula to clean a house in the village. There, she served doña Emilia, the wife of a government clerk who lived in one of the rare bungalows with an enclosed kitchen and tile roof. Paula felt grateful for the employment. She disliked being dependent on others, and her job as a maid contributed three dollars a week to the family. She gave Maximo all but thirty cents, which she tithed to the church. In addition to the money, she was thankful for the walk home from town. The time alone on the road granted her an opportunity to speak with Alberto, who met her at the crossroads and walked alongside her for almost an hour.

She took great care never to arrive home suspiciously late and her reputation remained unsmudged. No, there was nothing Rosendo could possibly know, because she guarded the hidden workings of her heart even from herself. The heart is desperately wicked, she believed. Who could know it?

Rosendo removed his hat, wiped his brow with a wrinkled handkerchief, and cleared his throat. "Well," he said, "I happen to know one secret."

"Are you a fortune-teller?" She rolled her eyes.

"You could say that."

"Then don't tell me. I'd rather not know it." Paula didn't believe in fortunes. She inched away from him, but he took a step closer, leaned down, and whispered into her ear.

"You, young lady, are about to make a disastrous mistake."

Her face paled with the sensation of his breath on her skin.

"I know you more than you think. The problem with you is you surround yourself with dreamers. Losers. Little boys in a world of men."

"What?" She shivered and stepped away. Their conversation had taken an uncomfortable turn.

He laughed and said, "God, you should see your face."

His tone was good humored, but she didn't like being laughed at.

Still smiling, he said, "To be honest, I saw you just now, standing here like a lost sheep, and I felt sorry for you, I really did. A young, beautiful girl alone in the world."

"I'm not alone." Paula turned for her friends, but the other girls had followed the band of musicians, who were making their way under an ornate balcony and toward the parade. Her eyes widened, flustered. To be seen talking alone with an older man, even if he was Alberto's older brother, jeopardized her reputation. "Maximo's very strict," she said. "I need to catch up with my friends."

He grinned. "You're terribly sweet. I can see why he likes you so much."

Paula fretted with the neck of her blouse. "Who? What are you talking about?"

"Alberto. He's told me all about you."

"He has?"

"Of course. You're his sweetheart, aren't you?"

She considered this and didn't know how to answer. Paula and Alberto had pretend-married as children. She held a bouquet of red *flor de maga*, flowers that looked like teacups in her tiny fist. He wore an undershirt and his father's sun-bleached fedora, faded, with a brown sweat ring around the rim. Barefooted, dirt-stained children. When he touched her hand as a girl, she didn't pull away. As children, they spent their afternoons on a hillside taking turns on a rope swing, leaping over dry gullies until they grew sticky with heat. To quench their thirst, Alberto would climb a nearby tree for ripe mangos, and they would sit overlooking the rooftops of the barrio as a stream of smoke billowed from the Fajardo Sugar Mill. Without a knife, they would bite through the thick mango skin like biting into apples, sweet juice dripping down their chins, strands of pulp sticking between their teeth.

In their village, parties and wedding ceremonies were uncommon. Few people could afford to host guests or pay for legal documents. Even had her parents been Catholics like most of her neighbors, there was no money for white dresses or small birthday gatherings, no *quinceañeras*. What little they had went to food, not X-rays, not medicine.

"I wouldn't call us sweethearts," she said. "But we are old friends."

"Then let's be friends, too," he said. "Family friends." Rosendo's voice sounded thick with rum, and he smiled. "While he's in Ponce, I think a chaperone would be appropriate."

"I don't need looking after."

"Of course not, but I do. Come on, keep me out of trouble."

She thought he was a *macho*, showing off, but she didn't say those things. Just then, something about his expression reminded her of Alberto. Maybe it was his smile. Apart from it, she saw little resemblance between the brothers. Head to head in height, Alberto was a leaner, darker version of this older brother.

"You don't look much like your brother."

"Half brothers," said Rosendo. "Alberto takes after his father, and I suppose I take after mine." He raised one eyebrow. "Other than that, we're practically twins."

Paula stammered. "I'm sorry. I'm not usually so rude, I didn't know."

"I'm not sorry," Rosendo said. "I left home when Alberto was only two. I was gone for a long time. I'd just come back when . . . that year your parents got sick. I wasn't home long. I took off again to get a spot on the cutting line with the *macheteros*. Now I work at the mill."

"You're lucky then. I heard, the mill swore off *Nacionalistas*. Ever since that strike three years ago."

"I'm no Nationalist," he said. "Don't confuse me with my baby brother. I don't give a damn about those *políticos*."

Paula's face darkened. "Don't tell me you're one of those Statehoodies."

"I'm not. I'm nothing," Rosendo said. "Here, sugar is king. I have no interest in marching up and down in ridiculous parades that amount to shit."

"Maybe, but the boys are serious around here," she said. "I mean it. They're calling for revolution."

"Revolution?" Rosendo sucked his teeth. "Chaos is all that is. No better than hungry spirits."

"What do you mean?"

He squinted his eyes at Paula. "What do you people think? Think the *Yanquis* are just going to swim back to *Yanquilandia*? Think they're going to hand the country over to a bunch of good-for-nothing schoolboys? It'll be a hell of a fight. Then what? Your revolutionary's gonna come in here and clean house, is that it? Nah, we both know how that ends."

"How could we possibly know?"

"Look, I might not be some schoolboy like Alberto, but I know about masters. The real kind. Get rid of one, and some other far worse is just chomping at the bit to step in, occupy."

His words reminded her of the parable of the unclean spirit's return. How after the house had been swept clean, seven other spirits, more evil than the first, moved right in. Politics. She didn't want to hear another word about it, but Rosendo's abrasive disregard for Alberto's work and the independence movement made her feel defensive. "There's always hope," she said.

"Don't be naïve. You sound like Alberto."

"And you sound like my brother Maximo," she said. "He says the *Nacionalistas* are bad for business."

Rosendo seemed to dig his heels in. "They are. What does your brother have to say of your Alberto enlisting with the cadets?"

"He's not *my* Alberto. He can do as he pleases. Besides, I never speak of him."

"Smart girl."

She was unaccustomed to compliments and smiled despite herself. "Thanks. Maximo doesn't like all this talk about Yankee imperialism. Says the radio is just stirring up trouble."

"He's right. They're rounding boys like Alberto up, right off the streets just for applauding at nationalist rallies? You hear all sorts of strange talk on the road. Rumors."

"Of course." She lowered her voice. She'd warned Alberto of these same risks herself, but hearing Rosendo speak them aloud with such certainty made her angry. "You think I don't know this? I read the papers. I hear the gossip about the *carpetas*." On the island, it was suspected that spies and informants kept tabs on *Independentistas*, feeding the secret police information about nationalist supporters.

"It's more than gossip. It's real and it's dangerous," said Rosendo.

Her stomach knotted. From the moment Alberto had mentioned the march in Ponce, she'd felt nervous. "It was nice seeing you again, señor Ortiz Cruz, but I really don't want to miss the parade."

"Not Ortiz," he corrected. "It's just Rosendo Cruz. Alberto's father was Ortiz, not mine. I never knew my father."

"He didn't give you his family's name?"

"No. But I hear I got his baby blues." He batted his long lashes and smiled a sardonic grin.

His eyes made her think of sea glass, waves, and currents.

To look even briefly into them pulled her deeper with undertow force.

"Don't rush off," he said.

She heard the Palm Sunday parade starting and glanced around, nervous and agitated that she'd miss the beginning. "I think the parade might start."

"And God forbid we miss it."

"Who doesn't like a good parade?

"Parades are good for one thing, and one thing only," he said. "Music, food, pretty girls, and collecting on a cock."

"That's more than one thing," she said.

He smiled. "I play the numbers. I don't count them."

"You mean gambling?" she said. "You sound sure of yourself."

"I am. I don't believe in luck," he said.

"Neither do I." She believed things happened for reasons, believed in God's insurmountable will. What did luck have to do with anything?

He tapped his temple. "It's not luck if it's a sure thing."

"So, you weren't kidding about the fortune-telling?"

"Let's just say, I don't lose."

"Ever?"

"You wouldn't understand. I can't explain my methods."

"Try me. You said I had a secret, right? What's yours?"

He stared at her for a long moment before speaking, as if assessing first if he could trust her. "Okay," he said. "But this is just between us." He lowered his voice and stepped closer. "Sometimes it's like I hear a voice."

"You hear voices?" She laughed, not at him so much as to combat her nerves.

"No, I said it's *like* a voice. Not a literal one, Jesus." He narrowed his eyes. "It's more like a color, a feeling in the pit of my gut. Sometimes it's a dream or a number in a dream."

The talk of dreams intrigued her. "What does it mean?"

"Means it's time to come into town and play the numbers or bet on a bird."

"Then what?"

He looked self-satisfied. "Then I sit back and collect."

"Collect? You mean you win? You make it sound so simple," she said. "If it's that easy, why aren't you a rich man?"

"Who says I'm not?"

She didn't answer, but cocked her eyebrows and took in his clothes as if to say, *It's obvious.*

"My problem is, I like to celebrate. You know what I mean?"

"Not really." She imagined him drinking, whoring with women. Her brother Maximo kept a strict house. He didn't step foot into bars, didn't play *bolita* numbers or watch cockfights, but she suspected Rosendo of all of those things and far worse. Being a strict Adventist, she'd learned to deny herself. Take up her cross. As a girl, she'd been raised to be silent, unseen. A negation of being. Now, she felt herself treading new territory, needing to show respect to Alberto's older brother all while maintaining her *dignidad.* She tried to sound aloof, to distance herself from him with her words. "I think your ideas of celebrating and mine are a little different."

"I'm not buying crocheted doilies, I'll tell you that much." His laughter was thunderous and from the throat. She noticed his small, white teeth and the way his laugh transformed his otherwise brooding features. "I have good instincts," he said. "Intuition. But it's certainly not enough to keep my ass off the cutting line. On a lucky day, I collect."

"And today? Is that why you're here, because of one of your dreamy wins?"

"Let's just say, it's a good day and leave it at that. You *will* keep my secret to yourself, right? I can trust you?" His tone was playful, but he looked at her conspiratorially.

"Old family friends, remember?" she said.

"That's right. That's exactly right." He nodded and sucked his teeth again. "I'm surprised Alberto abandons you like this. He should be more careful."

"He didn't abandon me," she said. "I can take care of myself."

"I'm sure you can. But if you don't mind, I'd feel more comfortable if I walked you to the parade." Rosendo gave a playful bow, tipping his hat toward Paula. "You know, I was born right here in Fajardo and spent the first eight years of my life in this village. Bet you didn't know that?"

"No, I didn't." She scanned the faces around her again, looking for an excuse to leave.

"Of course, how could you?" He grabbed a small bottle of cheap *cañita* rum out of his back pocket and took a long sip. "Now, no one recognizes me."

She noticed a flash of grief in his eyes before his expression reverted to cool stone. She now felt sorry for him. She could think of few things worse than being forgotten.

"You thirsty?" he said. "I could get you a drink."

"I don't drink." Her eyes were wide, fierce in her assessment of him. "Why did you choose to leave Fajardo?"

"Who said I had a choice?"

"I just thought . . ."

"Bastards don't get to choose," he said. "My stepfather wanted rid of me, so he sold me to a spiritist."

"Sold you?" She'd heard of families, desperate or vicious, who sold children into slavery but she'd also met Alberto's mother and couldn't imagine her capable of such things. Could Rosendo's words be true of her? "Did the woman mistreat you?"

"She wanted nothing more than a vessel, a medium for her *espiritismo*."

"What about your mother? Didn't she do something to try and stop your stepfather?"

"Not a damn thing."

"What happened?"

"I ran away."

"I know your mother Carmen," Paula said with some doubt. "She'd never do that."

"Apparently, you don't know her as well as you think."

"Come on, is that true?"

"There are no true stories," he said. "Only memories."

She felt sorry for him and said so, but he squinted and said he didn't want her pity. She said, "It sounds like the Lord protected you all those years, brought you finally home."

He lifted an eyebrow. "I brought myself." He sighed and said, "Do me a favor, let me treat a friend of the family. I could use another drink, and you could use a *piragua*. It's boiling out here."

Sweet cherry syrup over shaved ice on a sweltering day sounded like heaven. Still, she felt uncertain. What would people think if they saw her at the parade with a strange, older man? Someone would tell Maximo for sure. "I don't think so," she said.

"We'll wait for the parade together." He put his hands in his pockets and gave her a pleading look. "Don't insult me. It's my treat."

Years later, she would look back at her decision and teach her own daughters to follow their instincts, no matter what. "It's survival," she'd tell her girls. "If your gut tells you one thing and a man tells you another, trust your gut." But back then, she didn't know brokenness had its own magnetic force.

"Thank you," Paula said. "A piragua sounds nice." It was exactly what she wanted, but she tried to keep the desire out of her voice. She had no money of her own, so she didn't see the harm in accepting the treat and watching the parade with Alberto's older brother.

Rosendo led the way toward a peddler who gripped a chisel, hunched over a metal cart and shaving a block of ice. Women and children fanned themselves in the line that ran all the way to the steps of the municipal building.

Rosendo pulled the handkerchief out of his trouser pocket again and wiped his face. He paid five cents each for two large piraguas, and they grew quiet, focused on the task of licking the cherry ice from their paper cones. Syrup dripped down Paula's wrist.

"Careful, you'll ruin your nice skirt." Rosendo leaned against a heavy wooden door as he spoke. He dabbed the syrupy trail on her wrist with his thumb, then sucked the finger clean.

"It's my sister-in-law's," she said, inspecting it for red stains. "Borrowed."

All day, she had felt entirely plain, her old-fashioned, country skirt cinched at her waist while other girls her age wore their dresses low, resting on their hips. Luz Marí called Paula's black, unruly curls undignified, and forced the girl to wear her hair pinned up at the nape without even a bow. When she'd looked in the small mirror that morning, Paula had feared being mistaken for an old spinster although she was barely seventeen. Even Alberto didn't seem to notice her lately. Ever since Pedro Albizu Campos swore revenge for the police killings in Rio Piedras and called for the establishment of a nationalist military, Alberto thought of nothing else. Talked of nothing else. How could she blame him? He had set his eyes on a Goliath. She was just a distraction. She admonished herself for being selfish, vain.

"I bet you look better in it," Rosendo said.

"What?" she asked, distracted by the syrup dripping once again down the paper cone.

"The skirt suits you. I'd bet money your sister-in-law doesn't look half as nice in it."

She blushed and thanked him again. Her sister-in-law, five years older, with her sallow skin, pinched eyes, and willow limbs, looked twice her age. With the birth of each new child, her sister-in-law grew anemic and ill-tempered. Paula often found herself the brunt of the woman's spite, but instead of rebuke, she pitied Luz Marí. She recognized the distress of a woman teetering month by month to keep her children fed and clothed.

"From over there, we'll have a good view of the parade." Before she could answer, he grabbed her forearm and hustled her through the crowded plaza with its pastel-colored colonial buildings. It was difficult to keep up as he wound in and out of the path of pedestrians, men on horseback, and several automobiles. Already, a crowd had gathered to view the musicians, and Rosendo pressed between bodies to get a good view.

The villagers of Fajardo commemorated the *Domingo de Ramos,* the triumphal entry of Jesus Christ into Jerusalem. With palm branches in hand, congregants marched all the way from the cathedral steps and through the plaza.

Rosendo stood behind Paula so she could see over the cluster of heads. The crowd packed around her on all sides. Rosendo took a wide stance, grounding himself behind her, and he leaned into the curve of her back, his hand gently on her waist. His hips, shadow-like, rubbed against her. She froze. Confused, she shifted a centimeter away from him, but he slid with her, hemming her in, pressing harder.

Ashamed and embarrassed, she felt blood rush to her head, but she didn't dare turn and confront him. Could it be her imagination? She didn't want to overreact, cause a scene.

"Praise him! Praise him!" shouted the procession.

MOTHER SHIP

New York
1983

Esther received her *elekes* necklaces as a baby, and at age eight, her mother Isabel explained that the sacred bead necklaces were blessed and flowed with *ashé* power for protection. "These were prepared especially for you," her mother said. "They were bathed in a sacred herbal bath, and then they were fed." Her mother kissed the necklaces before slipping them over her neck. Esther didn't know what to make of the necklaces. How could she feed something that had no tongues, no lips, no teeth? Five altogether, each necklace represented a different *orisha*, the spirits who governed the elements of fire, water, air, and earth—all white beads for the purity of Obatalá, red and white for the warrior Changó, gold and orange for Oshún, blue and clear crystal for the queen of the sea Yemayá, and black and red for Eleguá.

Her *madrina*, Lourdes, wore an all-white dress and sang in an unrecognizable language. Her melodic voice rose and fell, filling the candlelit basement. She cast the coconut pieces to the ground, and said, "When you grow up, you will be a priestess like me. You are already halfway to becoming a saint." Esther imagined herself as a wooden figure carved and painted, forever stuck on a church shelf.

At ballet class, Esther remembered to keep her arms straight and her toes pointed in first arabesque. During her piano lesson, she remembered the word FACE to memorize the notes on a staff with a treble clef, and at home, she memorized the rules of the *elekes* necklaces:

1. Don't wear them in the bath.
2. Don't wear them to sleep.
3. If you take them off, kiss them and wrap them in a white cloth or hang them on a hook.
4. Kiss them before you put them on each morning.
5. Don't let anyone other than your mother or godmother touch them.

There were other rules, too, Madrina said. Rules for adults that she didn't have to worry about memorizing. Not yet. Her mother promised if Esther took good care of her *elekes*, she would buy her a Cabbage Patch Kid and a dollhouse for Christmas.

*

When her mother kissed Esther's necklaces and put them around her neck, Esther hoped to feel goose bumps from the top of her head to the tips of her toes. Her mother said, "Do you feel the *ashé*?" But Esther felt nothing. No power. No change. "People don't change overnight," her mother said. "It takes time."

In Saturday morning cartoons, He-Man the Master of the Universe raised his sword into the air and yelled, "By the power of Grayskull!" as lightning zapped the sky. Bolts of energy struck his sword and He-Man received power. Esther tucked her necklaces under the satin collar of her Pink Ladies jacket. "Go, Grease Lightning" looped repeatedly in her head. She wondered about the *ashé*, waiting for the moment when power would strike.

In a black-and-white Polaroid, Esther's mother wore a string bikini with tassels, high heels, and a beaming smile. She wielded beauty like a sword. "I had such big eyes, everyone used to call me Twiggy," her mother said.

Esther held the photograph close to her face and said, "You look like a movie star." On her lap, she rested a needlepoint cushion, and on top of the cushion was a steaming plate of buttery macaroni and broccoli.

Her mother balanced a cigarette between her lips and plucked the photo out of Esther's hand. "Ay, *nena*, don't touch it with your dirty fingers." Her mother slipped the photograph back inside the clear plastic jacket of the album and told Esther that she had been the only girl on her mother's block who had danced in the Puerto Rican Day parade.

Esther said, "You looked really pretty."

"You know it. I could've gone to the High School of the Performing Arts."

"Like *Fame*?" Esther blew on her fork before each bite, and wiped butter from her chin with the back of her arm.

"Use a napkin, Miss Piggy." Her mother lifted a paper towel from the coffee table and tossed it beside Esther's lap.

Esther ate the macaroni, but ignored the broccoli in a corner of the plate. "I'm full," she said.

"No way, you eat every bite."

The girl scowled, but put a stalk of the cold broccoli in her mouth and chewed.

When Esther complained about bedtime or refused to eat vegetables, her mother told her the story of El Cuco, a bogeyman who was a child eater and a kidnapper. Esther's face soured and tears rolled down her cheeks as she gagged on the broccoli. Still, she ate every bite. El Cuco took the shape of shadows, hid under beds. He ate disobedient children, devouring them whole. Left no trace.

When the network television movie *Adam* premiered, it aired after Esther's bedtime. Scared of the dark, the girl padded into her parents' bedroom clutching a pillow to her chest.

The television illuminated the dark room with a radiant blue glow. Covered in a pile of thick blankets, only her mother's head was visible on the sheets. Her father's side of the bed was empty as usual. He worked late shifts as a pharmacist and was rarely home before eleven.

"Can I sleep here?" Esther asked. "I had a bad dream."

"Oh, God, you and your ridiculous dreams. You can't be doing this every night. You know that right? You're too old for this shit."

"I know."

"You're lucky I don't march you right back to your room, young lady, and get the Vicks."

Esther sucked in a deep breath, frozen. Just the threat of Vicks smeared across her eyelids was enough to make her eyes water.

"All right," her mother said. "But this is the last time."

Esther nodded.

"Take that blanket." Her mother pointed to a rose-covered quilt at the foot of the bed. "You can sleep on the love seat, but I don't want to hear another peep out of you, got that? It's late."

Esther grabbed the cotton quilt from the foot of the bed and wrapped it around her shoulders like a shawl. She loved to sleep on the loveseat in her parents' room, an ornate Victorian chaise lounge upholstered in amethyst velvet. During the day, she pretended to faint on the lounge. Over and over again, she imagined herself graceful and delicate, a meek princess awaiting a Sleeping Beauty kiss. She practiced the kiss on the back of her hand, practiced the precise way her lashes would flutter when she opened her eyes. The great awakening, the rescue.

At night, she preferred the chaise lounge to her own bed. She liked the secure feeling of being cocooned in the blue haze of the television. Her mother forced Esther to sleep with her back to the screen, but the girl would watch in the reflection of the palm-sized oak vanity from her dollhouse. That's how she first heard about Adam Walsh. Watching through the tiny reflection in the vanity mirror, she saw little Adam who had disappeared from a Sears Department Store in Hollywood, Florida. In a photo, he proudly posed with his baseball bat and his red cap, his toothless grin. So small yet larger than life itself. Vanished without a trace until police found his head in the Vero Canal.

There is no telling why some stories slip into the crevices of your bones, fuse like grafted stems into your own story. That's how

Esther felt about Adam. He was only three months younger than her, and he looked like every boy in her class. The same two front teeth that were missing from Adam's smile were missing from hers.

In the television series *Get Smart*, secret agent Maxwell Smart and Agent 99 worked for a U.S. government agency known as *CONTROL*. Together, they fought their evil nemesis KAOS. In car pools, Esther and four other children from City Island drove past Public School 175 and over the City Island Bridge, past Orchard Beach to attend the more prestigious elementary school in Larchmont, an upscale community in Westchester County. Westchester, one of the richest counties in the nation, was worth the twenty-minute commute and the fortune in extra property taxes. Larchmont, with its pristine golf courses, yacht clubs, and tree-lined cul-de-sacs practically guaranteed high SAT scores and college scholarships.

Esther thought her car pool smelled of stale apple juice, and no matter which mom sat behind the wheel, all four unbuckled kids scrunched on the backseat floorboard, ducking out of sight from any potential KAOS agents. Esther slipped off her Reebok high-top, held the sole to her ear, and spoke into the heel.

"Hello CONTROL central. This is Special Agent Esther. Can you hear me? We are being followed. This is not a drill. I repeat, this is not a drill."

KAOS followed the car pool to and from school each and every day. Agents posed as employees at the Luncheonette Diner and the Penny Candy. They blended into shadows like El Cuco.

It was around this time that Esther began to see disfigured faces in reflections. For her, every mirror and window held specters looking back at her from the glass. Shadowy creatures walked the telephone lines like tight ropes, they crunched in corners and squatted under chairs. She squeezed her eyes shut, forcing them to vanish, but even the blackness behind her eyelids morphed into unspeakable horrors she couldn't unsee. The faces, along with the facts in her young life, blurred and slipped. She couldn't distinguish between the things she intensely imagined and the things that were real. It was like trying on her Grandma Paula's thick reading glasses and gently accepting a ruinous world all out of focus.

On her living room walls, a collection of decorative ebony masks hung above the fireplace. "For the masquerades," her mother said. Esther imagined that far across the Atlantic, elaborate masquerade rituals told stories of a great orchestrated illusion. Players and plays. There, disguised faces spoke of hidden realities just below the surface of skins, and if she listened carefully, Esther could hear the masks knocking their wooden teeth.

On occasion, Esther accompanied her mother at night to make the Ebo sacrificial offerings on the opposite side of the island. The Victorian houses on King Avenue sat dark and still behind picket fences, and these houses had views of Pelham Bay. Her mother would drive slowly past several houses with clapboard siding and brick chimneys before she'd stop the car in front of the old Pelham Cemetery gates. On this particular fall morning, she didn't cut the engine off. She just shifted into park and sat in silence for a moment, gripping the wheel with both hands. "I'll pop the trunk," her mother said. "Be quick."

Esther knew the cemetery well. Each year, an island-wide Halloween parade marched down City Island's main street at dusk and culminated at the cemetery's arched gates. Kids and parents from every block on the island gathered in costumes, carrying pillowcases of candy and cardboard UNICEF boxes, collecting coins for Ethiopia. By nightfall, all the trick or treating children crowded in front of the cemetery's iron gates hoping to catch a glimpse of dead Civil War soldiers creeping behind the tombstones. The kids screamed and laughed, and if they were lucky, a ghost pelted them with candy.

Now, the cemetery was empty. Esther heard the trunk pop before she said, "What if someone sees me?"

"Everyone's asleep," her mother said.

"That's not true." Esther looked out the car's back window. The sidewalk lay dark and deserted. She didn't want to get out of the car, not alone. And she didn't want to have to touch whatever lay inside the trunk.

Her mother shut off the headlights, but kept the engine running. "Go on," she said.

Esther zipped her jacket and pulled the hood over her ears and hair. Soft beads of rain tipped her nose and lashes. She wrapped her arms tightly around her chest, and walked toward the back of her mother's red Pontiac Trans Am. Inside the trunk sat a plastic bundle. It looked like something stuffed in a grocery bag and knotted on one end. She poked the bag. It felt soft, fleshy.

The bag was lighter and heavier than she had expected. She gripped it with her fingertips and held it away from her chest, hustling to the gates. She saw the tombs scattered along the grass, the bare branches stripping their dead leaves. She felt the piercing chill coming off the bay and heard the lapping of water.

She squinted her eyes and looked through the gate. The wind rustled the damp leaves at her feet and her hair whipped into her mouth.

Her mother leaned over and rolled down the passenger window. "What the hell are you waiting for? Throw the damn thing already."

Esther swung the bundle above her head, but with a soft thud it fell directly at her feet.

She heard her mother say from inside the car, "You've got to be kidding me."

Esther lifted the bag for a do-over, hoping it hadn't torn open. This time, she bent her knees and tossed it with both hands, like a basketball aiming for a hoop. She didn't wait for the sack to land a second time. She just ran, slammed the trunk closed, and dove into the car.

Her mother hit the gas and flicked on the headlights, a sly expression playing at the corners of her mouth.

*

In the 1983 miniseries *V,* an alien mother ship hovered over New York City, promising peace. The Visitors' high commander said they had landed on Earth for water and valuable minerals, and in exchange, the aliens offered the gift of advanced technology. Esther, too, considered her *elekes* to be a type of protective technology lost on modern science.

That Christmas her mother refused to get out of bed. It was as if all the air had been sucked from the house. Familiar with her mother's mood swings, Esther made a tremendous effort to sound festive, but her voice cracked. The bedroom felt claustrophobic, and dry heat radiated from the electric heater on the carpet. Esther stood at the cliff face of her mother's silence and forced a pleading smile. "Don't you want to get up? It's Christmas."

In Puerto Rico, Christmas was celebrated with huge *parrandas*, family and neighbors wearing *jíbaro* straw hats, caroling from house to house. It meant a roaming parade, growing as it went, the *parranderos* strumming guitars, shaking maracas, beating tambourines, and singing. It meant eating *lechón asao, pasteles,* and getting drunk on *coquito.* It meant pushing back the couches to make room for the musicians and the salsa dancers in the living room until dawn.

But by the time Esther was born, the Cruz family had left that world behind. Grandma Paula had come to New York in 1950 during what they all called The Great Migration, and after three decades of living in the city, the Cruz family had no men left. The men scattered, were drafted into the military, the gangs, the prisons. It was the peak of the AIDS epidemic, and along the Harlem River Drive, the graffiti read *Crack is Wack* above the highway like a resounding totem.

This was the same year real estate investors were invading everything between the Bowery and the East River to develop posh art galleries and luxury co-ops. The year a notice on Grandma Paula's door offered to pay seven thousand dollars to the tenants with rent control. So, as a sixty-three-year-old widow, Grandma Paula's life had come full circle. She decided she was tired of the burned-out buildings, the junkies, and the rat holes, and she moved back to Fajardo. With her, she pulled the rest of her family like a gravitational force, and just like that, the family of Cruz women packed up and left the city in a mass exodus, leaving Esther and her mother far behind.

In her mother's bedroom, Esther's mother didn't answer her questions. She didn't even blink. When she finally did speak, her voice sounded as if it had been pried loose from a rusted-out car. "Open the gifts without me."

Esther didn't want to open the gifts alone. "I can wait," she said.

"I'll be downstairs in a minute." Her mother turned her back and faced the wall.

In moments like these, Esther hated being an only child, the only witness. Like previous years, her dad had left that morning before sunrise without saying goodbye. The grandfather clock at the end of the hall donged ten times, and Matilda barked and scratched at the backdoor.

"Let the dog out," her mother said as Esther left the bedroom. "And close my door."

*

In *V*, after the ships had landed on earth, people voluntarily surrendered their freedom to the Visitors. What they didn't realize was that under the Visitors' thin mask of human-skin lived lizard creatures with forked tongues, creatures who planned to harvest humans for lunch.

Esther closed her mother's door behind her and felt exhausted, too. She imagined grabbing her mother's ear and pulling with a single, determined tug. She imagined the thin layer of olive skin lifting from sideburns to jaw. Below the skin, a face all green.

At the foot of the stairs, Matilda wagged her tail. Esther scratched behind the dog's ears before opening the French doors. A rush of dry air stung her face and chilled the tile under her sockless feet. Sleet crystalized over the yard, covered the dock, and the sky, an empty gray, smudged over the slate-colored Long Island Sound.

Through the glass doors, she watched Matilda crunch through week-old snow and squat. Matilda returned, panting clouds of breath, and Esther wiped each paw dry with a paper towel.

With a bowl of Rice Krispies on her lap, Esther sat crisscross at the base of the Christmas tree, staring blankly at the white twinkle lights, disinterested. The ten-foot tree was decorated with pink balls, lace ornaments, and silk ribbon. A white porcelain angel in a silver gown tipped the ceiling with her blond hair, and beneath the tree, gifts piled one on top of the other, wrapped in Santa Claus paper, spilling off the crocheted tree skirt.

None of the gifts needed labels. Every box had been wrapped for Esther.

Two hours later, her mother came down the stairs in her bathrobe, her eyes swollen and creased with smudged eyeliner. She said, "What are you waiting for?" Her voice sounded flat, alien. She knotted her bathrobe and walked into the kitchen. Standing next to the Mr. Coffee Maker, she lit a cigarette and watched the drips.

The gifts from Esther's mother were elaborate, beyond generous. Frilly pink dresses Esther would never wear, adult-size diamond studs, an amethyst birthstone necklace set in gold.

Her mother said, "What's wrong? You don't like them?" She leaned against the back wall, cupping a steaming mug with both hands.

"I do," Esther said. "It's just . . ." She looked down at the floor. She hadn't wanted anything in particular. She hadn't asked for gifts. The problem was that none of the gifts seemed intended for her. They weren't her style or taste, nor did they reflect her personality at all. It seemed as if the gifts had been picked out for another girl altogether.

"Just what?" her mother said, irritated.

Esther saw the disappointment on her mother's face. "I don't know. It's not a big deal. It's just, I don't really wear dresses anymore. Especially not pink."

"I know. That was the point. I'm sick of seeing you in ratty old jeans full of holes. You look like a bum."

"But I like my jeans. They're comfortable."

"You're just a kid. What do you know about style?" Her mother grabbed a garbage bag from under the sink and started shoving crinkled giftwrap into the bag. "It's fine, I'll take them back. I can take everything back. Jesus, you're thankless," she said. "Just like your father."

THE HOUSE OF THE SAINTS

New York
1974

Lourdes grabbed an aerosol room freshener from her shelf with the label *Go Away Evil* and began spraying it around the office. Isabel wrinkled her nose and sneezed.

Lourdes handed her a tissue and said, "You'll see. *Si del cielo te caen limones, aprende á hacer limonada.*"

Isabel blotted at the tears in her eyes. "I don't know how I can ever repay you for your help."

"In cash is best. I no longer accept personal checks, nothing personal."

*

The first initiation, called the *collares*, meant Isabel would receive necklaces for protection. Lourdes said that if she wanted victory over her life, the road would take sacrifice, and the sacrifice wouldn't be easy. Life fed on life, and the spiritual guides needed to be fed.

"Whatever you say, I'm ready," said Isabel.

"Good," said Lourdes. "Start with *collares*. But remember, it's all or nothing."

Isabel nodded in agreement, though her mind raced. What if her older sister Rosa was right? What if Lourdes really was a witch? What if spells made things worse? "I'm ready," she said. How else could she guarantee Jude's love or the family she so desperately wanted? Each momentary blessing felt tentative, as if they could be snatched away in an instant. She didn't deserve any of it, she thought. *You're no good, worthless, unlovable*, looped in her mind and the words had a life of their own.

She felt genuinely thankful for Lourdes' take-charge manner. She found her maternal warmth comforting. The woman had a way of looking at Isabel's face without judgment or ridicule, as if she looked beyond the surface and saw her true self.

"The first ceremony is just the beginning," said Lourdes. "It's like a baptism."

"I've already been baptized," said Isabel. "As a baby."

"No, that kind was different. I'm talking baptized into the mysteries and secrets of our faith, the faith of your ancestors."

"I guess I could do that."

"There's no guessing," Lourdes said. "You better make up your mind, and I mean quick. You've gotta know. I'm talking life-long commitment. This is bigger than your husband or your baby. There's no going back after today, you understand?"

Lourdes scrolled through a rolodex on her desk, pulling out index cards with names and phone numbers. "Baby steps, honey."

"I'll do anything," said Isabel.

Lourdes explained that Santeria was about serving the *orishas*. It was a pact. By serving them, the *orishas* were required to help. With Lourdes' guidance, Isabel could learn to govern them, and thereby, to take control of her own destiny.

"First we must ask the *orishas*," she said. "See if you can handle it. The Saints choose you, not the other way around. They know best. Don't you worry, sweetheart, they know just what you need." Lourdes picked up the receiver of the rotary telephone and began to dial.

*

Around noon, Lourdes flipped the sign on the shop's front door to *Closed*, and she and Isabel walked into the back office and through a door that entered Lourdes's living room. Lourdes lived behind the botanica in a three-bedroom apartment with her husband. Her adult children, grown and married, lived scattered throughout the five boroughs, but photos of children and grandchildren hung on every wall. Lourdes excused herself to change into a fresh white blouse and long white skirt, and told Isabel to make herself comfortable.

Soon men and women also dressed in head-to-toe white began arriving. They carried casserole dishes in their arms and plates of delicious-smelling foods. Isabel could smell fried fish and fresh bread. Her stomach growled. She couldn't remember the last time she'd felt like eating.

While one of the women lit candles around the room, Lourdes directed the guests to place the food on a large table covered in white linen. When Ernesto arrived wearing white dress pants and a white *guayabera*, Lourdes clapped her hands enthusiastically, a Christmas-morning expression in her eyes.

She patted Isabel's back. "Now we can start," she said.

In his traditional Caribbean shirt, with its vertical pleats and front pockets, Ernesto appeared elegant and serious. There was something regal and comforting about his expression, a glint of playful mischief in his eyes. To Isabel, he appeared taller than she remembered. Perhaps the candlelight played tricks on her eyes, or perhaps it was the way the other devotees greeted him with reverence, calling him *Baba*, father, and even bowing face down at his feet.

Isabel didn't know how to address him. What was the proper etiquette? As Ernesto approached her, she considered for a second crouching to the ground like the others, but didn't know the rules for outsiders.

"*Bendición*," she said quietly.

"Child, you look tired," he said as he kissed her cheek.

"Thank you for coming," she said.

He squeezed her hand. "Today you will receive the *collares* and start on the path you were destined for from the very beginning."

All her life, people had dismissed her. Here, Ernesto and Lourdes spoke of her destiny. Spoke about her life as if it had been predestined for greatness. They'd chosen her. In her, they saw something special. She desperately wanted to believe they were right.

Isabel nodded. "I'm ready."

A young man entered the room holding cages in each arm. Ernesto motioned him closer with a wave. "Isabel, this is one of our newest godsons, Tomás."

Tomás stood silent, shyly assessing her. Inside his cages, he held a pair of chickens and a pair of pigeons. Ernesto placed his hands on her shoulders. When he spoke, he tilted his head to peer at her through his one clear, gray eye. "Lourdes honors me by asking me to assist her with your initiation. This is an exciting day for us all, coming together to witness your birth. This doesn't happen every day, you know. Many consult the *orishas*, but only a few are chosen into the family."

"I'm excited, too," she said, sounding more nervous than she had intended.

"Not everyone is called to receive the *collares*," said Tomás. "Congratulations."

"Thank you," she said. "I came here seeking damage control because of my many mistakes in life, but everyone seems to be congratulating me for some reason." She laughed timidly, but when she noticed no one else laughing, she forced a serious, somber expression. "I don't know what to make of it all."

"The *orishas* have their ways of drawing all of us," said Tomás. "Sometimes it's straight through rock bottom."

Ernesto grinned at him with the pride of a father. "*Ahijado*, please hurry back to the car and bring the caged possum." Tomás excused himself and walked to the kitchen with the caged birds.

"I hope you are certain," said Ernesto. "You are about to awaken into a world of unbelievable power."

In the kitchen, a woman named Toñita was busy chopping and slicing a coconut. Another woman introduced as Lydia handed Isabel a Caldor's department store bag. Lourdes instructed Isabel to use the bathroom to change into the new clothes. Inside the bag, Isabel found a white summer dress. The tags were still on the out-of-season dress, marked down seventy percent. Isabel didn't want to get out of her jeans and warm sweater, but she did as she was told and changed.

Some of the women chatted casually with mugs of coffee in their hands.

"You look cold," said one of the women, as Isabel emerged in the sundress. She handed Isabel a mug of steaming coffee.

"Thank you." She took the mug and sipped. Had all these people gathered just to help her? She didn't know what to make of the many guests dressed in white, the food, or the caged animals. "Who are all these people?" she asked Lourdes.

Lourdes explained that some of the guests were Ernesto's godchildren, but most were her own. She said some ceremonies required the special skills of *Babalawos*, and Ernesto had come to celebrate and give Isabel guidance for her future. The others had come to help with her initiation, to show support. "Soon you will be part of our *Ilé*, family," said Lourdes. She explained that from that day forward, Isabel would always be welcome in her *casa de santos*. "The first day we met, you walked into my shop an *aleyo*, an outsider. When we're finished with you, you'll be leaving an *ahijada*, a goddaughter."

Isabel looked appreciatively at the people around her, her new brothers and sisters.

Lourdes gestured toward the gathering and said, "Meet your new family."

Isabel smiled. It felt like a fraternity of secrets, and she was hopeful for the first time in months.

Ernesto stood beside a table, gripping a hammer. "We will initiate you with the *elekes*, the necklaces. Then you will receive the three Warrior spirits—Eleguá, Ogun, and Ochosi. They will protect you against all evil."

He smashed the hammer down on a coconut, splitting the hard shell with a loud crack. He gathered the milk into a glass and set the meaty white pieces aside. With a kitchen knife, he probed the white and brown rings, cutting them into uneven squares.

Lourdes leaned close to Isabel's ear and whispered, "Eleguá always comes first." In the center of the room, Ernesto placed a stone on the floor. Its shape was like a head. Where the eyes, ears, and mouth should have been, there were smooth cowrie shells.

"This stone represents the *orisha* called Eleguá," Lourdes said. She explained that Eleguá opened and closed all doors, so they honored him first because they needed his permission to open the doors of communication with the other *orishas*.

Ernesto sprinkled drops of water from a glass labeled *Holy Water*. He dipped the coconut rings into the glass. With his fingernail, he sliced slivers of coconut and placed the flecks in front of Eleguá. "He is first to be fed," he said.

Isabel said, "Like real food? It eats?"

Ernesto nodded. "Yes, like an offering. Great power requires great energy, so we offer food and blood to sustain their need for energy. Feeding the *orishas* is one of our most important acts of service."

The devotees gathered around Ernesto as he worked, and Tomás stood in the outer circle beating a rapid rhythm on an hourglass-shaped drum. Drumming filled the candlelit room, fusing the gathering into one unified pulse. Moving to the drums felt instinctive. Isabel didn't have to think, her body knew exactly what to do, and she and the others moved as one, swaying to the tempo as it increased in speed. Somehow, the beating of the drum reverberated in her whole body, till she no longer felt her body. Instead she felt connected, like one body, with everyone else in the room.

"We are enticing the *orishas* to come," said Ernesto. His eyes widened, excited. "Can you feel it?"

Isabel did feel it. She felt the atmosphere in the room shift and vibrate, as if she were standing on the precipice between two worlds.

In the corner of the room stood a cauldron. Isabel couldn't see what was inside the cauldron, but she caught a glimpse of metal and bone.

"Focus," Lourdes reprimanded. "Repeat after me."

Isabel repeated the words as Lourdes chanted an invocation to the soft beat of the drum.

Holding the coconut rings in his hands, Ernesto touched the floor in front of the stone head of Eleguá and made the sign of the cross. He finished the invocation of blessing and dispelled the evil influences. Then he asked aloud if Isabel was permitted to receive the *collares* for protection. He threw the coconut rinds to the ground. All of the coconut pieces fell white facing up.

Lourdes smiled, "*Alafia.*" She stood beside Ernesto and both kissed the floor. "Eleguá says yes." She looked elated. "He says, yes!"

"We will now cast the coconuts and read the patterns," said Ernesto. "In this way, we consult the *Egun.*"

"Who?" Isabel was fluent in Spanish, but so many of the words they spoke were Yoruban and unfamiliar to her. "Who are the *Egun?*"

"The dead," said Ernesto.

For several minutes, yes and no questions were asked, coconut pieces were cast, and the answers were announced. With each new question, Ernesto touched the rinds to the ground several times and prayed. Then he stood upright, clasped the rinds to his chest, and released them to the floor. They scattered, an oracle to be read. "You are the daughter of Yemayá, goddess of the ocean, and your daughter inside you is a child of Oshún, goddess of rivers." His eyes gleamed, and the godchildren in the room clapped and patted Isabel on the back.

Coconut rinds fell on top of each other. Ernesto sprinkled holy water over the rinds, then offered the water glass to Isabel to drink. "It's rare to see so many *ire* in one session," he said, still smiling.

"Ire?" Isabel repeated, confused.

"It means 'good luck,'" said Lourdes.

Ernesto gave Isabel's hand a tender squeeze. "You have been especially blessed."

Isabel felt encouraged by the ceremony. The guests in the room nodded their heads in agreement. Some shook her hand and kissed her cheek.

Tomás leaned into her ear and whispered, "You're blessed."

Others congratulated her on her initiation and told her she was very powerful. *We'll teach you to work those powers of yours, don't you worry.* And just like that, Isabel felt as if she'd stumbled onto a beautiful secret, uncovered a hidden strength. She felt united with the people in the room, as if she belonged somewhere for the very first time in her entire life.

When the proper time came, everyone knelt while Ernesto held a chicken by its legs and waved it over the heads of the devotees. For Isabel, he passed the chicken over her whole body, wiping her with its feathers. She cringed, but Lourdes explained that it wiped away evil and impurities. "Be still," she said.

Ernesto windmilled the bird in the air, and with a swift twist, he broke the chicken's neck. For a few horrible seconds it flapped and kicked, but he suspended the bird by its legs to let the blood drain to the neck before slicing its throat.

"Don't be scared," Lourdes said. "There's no pain."

Ernesto plucked several feathers from the bird's chest and dipped the feathers in blood, before touching Isabel's forehead with them.

"Flesh and blood restores the divine energy to the saints," Ernesto said. "Sometimes we cook the meat and have a feast, but when blood removes impurities, we discard the animal."

The ceremony of the coconuts ended and people began to clean and care for the sacred objects. Everyone seemed to have a task except for Isabel, who was told to follow Lourdes upstairs. At the top of the stairs, Isabel noticed that the bedroom to the left held no furniture minus one wicker chair. The chair was in the center of the room and faced the door. The bedroom to the right was furnished with a queen-size bed and wooden dresser. Above the dresser, a white sheet was draped over the mirror. Isabel was directed into the bedroom and noticed the window also had a white sheet draped over the glass. The bathroom was connected to this bedroom and Lourdes led the way. Here too the mirror of the medicine cabinet was draped with a white sheet.

"Why are all the mirrors covered?" asked Isabel.

"The world of the *orishas* is like a big cosmic mirror." Lourdes pressed her palms together to illustrate her point. "The coming together of two worlds," she said. "The crossroads." She said they covered the mirrors because some of the new initiates were not permitted to look into mirrors for an entire year. They had undergone a major initiation known as *Asiento*, or the making of the saint, and they had to abide by many rules.

"What about me? What's my next step?" said Isabel.

"First, we baptize you," said Lourdes. The bathroom had a porcelain tub already half filled with water. "To represent new birth."

The muscles in Isabel's body tightened. She wanted to trust Lourdes, did trust her, but the idea of standing naked and exposed made her feel vulnerable. Isabel tried to not think of her body, tried to focus on the white sheet over the mirror.

Lourdes pulled up her thin, summer dress and slipped the fabric over Isabel's head. It lay in a heap on the bath mat along with her bra and panties. Isabel squeezed her eyes tighter and listened as Lourdes chanted.

With surprising strength for a middle-aged woman, Lourdes lifted Isabel off her feet and placed her in the tepid water. Isabel sat with her back facing the woman, and Lourdes cupped palms of water and dripped the water over Isabel's head, shoulder, and back. Lourdes scrubbed Isabel's skin with a brittle bar of soap and chanted in a smooth, singsong voice. Isabel hugged her legs to her chest as fresh tears streamed down her cheeks.

"I don't even know why I'm crying anymore," Isabel said, laughing and crying at the same time.

"Tears come at every birth," Lourdes said, and as she scrubbed at Isabel's skin, she seemed to be scratching at scabby bits of consciousness, opening fresh wounds. Isabel kept her eyes shut, not wanting to see her own nakedness or the woman's hands on her bare skin. She tried to focus on the words in the air between them like a blinding cloud, numbing the shame and the strange feeling of loss.

Lourdes helped Isabel out of the tub and draped her in a new white towel before redressing her in her white undergarments and summer dress. There was a knock at the bathroom door, and a woman entered, carrying a tray. One plate on the tray held the pieces of coconut from the earlier ceremony. Other plates had cocoa butter, toasted corn, bits of smoked fish, and dried possum. Isabel didn't see the second woman behind the first, but she handed Lourdes a live chicken in a cardboard box and the stone head of Eleguá. In silence, the items were placed on the bathroom floor, and the women retreated downstairs.

Lourdes locked the knob and draped a white sheet over the bathroom door. She placed the stone head of Eleguá in the center of the bathroom, and she and Isabel stood facing the face made of shells. Without warning, Lourdes lifted the gray and white speckled chicken and placed it in Isabel's arms.

"Please don't tell me I have to kill it." Isabel held the chicken away from her body, stiff and afraid. She'd never held a living chicken before with her hands. It rustled its feathers and shook.

"Stand still," snapped Lourdes. "Don't insult Eleguá. This could go very bad for you yet."

Isabel was surprised by Lourdes's sharp tone, but she saw a hint of fear in the woman's eyes. She felt the sting of the reprimand and stopped fidgeting, eyeing the bird's sharp beak.

"Eleguá, do you want the blood of this chicken?" Lourdes tossed the coconut rings to the ground. "He says, yes." With a swift motion, Lourdes twisted the chicken's neck, tearing the head off with her palm.

Blood dripped on the stone head and over the floor. Lourdes dipped her finger into a honey jar and sucked the finger clean. She dipped her finger a second time and offered the honey finger to Isabel. "Taste," she said. Isabel parted her lips over the finger and sucked. The gesture was intimate, and Isabel trembled with uncertainty. Then Lourdes poured honey over the blood and plucked chicken feathers from the headless bird, scattering the feathers over the blood and honey.

Lourdes held several feathers and mixed the blood and honey. "Now you," she said.

Isabel plucked more feathers from the bird and imitated Lourdes.

The ceremony concluded with the *roacion de cabeza*, the cleansing of the head. Lourdes placed grated coconut on Isabel's head, said more prayers, and lit more candles. Then her head, coconut and all, was wrapped in a stiff white towel.

The first of the *collares* presented to Isabel was the white beaded necklace of Obatalá. Lourdes kissed the necklace before draping it over Isabel's toweled head.

"He is father of the gods," said Lourdes, explaining that the *orisha* Obatalá was the saint of peace, harmony, and purity. He represented clarity, justice, and wisdom. "Everything white belongs to him," she said.

Lourdes kissed the second beaded necklace, made of white and blue beads, and placed it over Isabel's head. "This necklace belongs to our mother Yemayá." She said Yemayá was the goddess of the sea and the provider of wealth. When they attended church, they called her The Virgin Mary, but when they were at sea, they called her Yemayá, the mermaid.

Oshún's necklace was all yellow. "Oshún is daughter of Yemayá and Orungan." She said Oshún was the goddess of love and gold, and the teacher of pleasure.

The white-and-red-beaded necklace belonged to Changó, god of fire, thunder, and lightning. "He is our mighty warrior. With his help, you'll overcome your enemies. Dominate." Lourdes said each spirit had a Catholic counterpart, and in time, Isabel would learn the secret identity of all the *orishas*.

"For example, Changó is the patron Saint Barbara," said Lourdes.

"But I thought Changó was male. Why a woman saint?"

"Well, Changó disguises himself as a woman to hide from his enemies. In church, we light a candle to Saint Barbara, but deep down, we're really saying prayers to Changó."

Lourdes said she was a daughter of Yemayá, initiated in the mysteries of the goddess of the sea, and she had the power to initiate others. "It's like giving birth," she said. "Today, you received the *collares*, the first initiation. Now you're on the road to becoming a Santera. I give birth to you. That makes me your godmother."

"Me, a Santera? But how?"

"The making of a saint is a long journey. It could take years and lots of money. Thousands of dollars. But what you get back in return is priceless."

"I'll do it," said Isabel.

Lourdes placed her hand on Isabel's shoulder and patted her like a petulant child. "I know you're anxious, dear, but to do santo is a serious decision. There is a lot to learn about our practice and our etiquette of secrecy. When you begin down this road, it is forever."

"Whatever it takes," said Isabel. "I want this."

"You're eager, and that's good. But you let your emotions control you, and that's dangerous. Lifting the veil before you're protected and ready jeopardizes your mental and physical health. This is a journey, not a race. But don't worry. I'm your teacher now, and I'm the best." Lourdes smiled, and the two women descended the stairs, the godmother and her newly initiated goddaughter.

Lourdes leaned into Isabel's ear and spoke. "From this day forward, I will be the most important person in your life."

DUST TO DUST

Puerto Rico
1937

Paula walked along the foothills of the Luquillo Range, a mountain ridge named after a Taíno chief, and crossed a dirt road dotted with little shacks made of corrugated cardboard and scraps of tin. Barefoot children sprinted past her, howling and shouting toward a filthy stream. Old men sat on wood crates in front of their homes, eyeing her with curiosity.

When Paula arrived at doña Emilia's bungalow to clean, she found the woman sitting pale-faced at the kitchen table, her breakfast uneaten. Beside her plate and coffee mug sat the family radio, blaring.

"What's wrong? Is everything all right?" Paula placed a gentle hand on the elderly woman's shoulder.

"*Siéntate, mija. La información es muy grave.*"

Never before had the doña invited Paula to sit at her table, but the look of terror in her watery eyes was enough for Paula to pull up a chair and listen. Then she heard it. The radio announced the news of a Palm Sunday clash between Nationalists and police in Ponce.

At first, Paula couldn't grasp what she'd heard. The radio reporter spoke of nationalist snipers and police acting in self-defense. It made no sense. Alberto had said the cadets were marching in a peaceful demonstration. It was a parade, not a riot.

As the broadcast continued, Paula imagined Alberto and the other cadets, some as young as fifteen, standing in formation on

Calle Marina, proud and ready to step off into the parade. She imagined the excitement of the energized crowd, the waving and applauding, the Nurses Corp lined up behind the men. Her chest expanded as she envisioned a triumphal entry worthy of Palm Sunday.

Her brother had called the Nationalists fanatics, but he was wrong. Alberto was a believer, yes, but he was levelheaded, good-tempered.

She didn't breathe. Hard of hearing, doña Emilia had the volume at full blast. Even so, Paula leaned closer to the speakers. The voice on the radio swallowed the small kitchen whole, until the walls fell away. It described the band playing the patriotic "La Borinqueña," as a young cadet of the republic in his black shirt, black cap, and white trousers waved the Puerto Rican flag. Another cadet waved the flag of the French Revolutionaries, the adopted flag of the Puerto Rican Nationalist Party. From the bystanders, there was shouting. *¡Viva Puerto Rico Libre! ¡Libertad! Down with the colonial pirates.*

Young boys pumped their fists into the air chanting, "Free *El Maestro*," the nickname for their leader Pedro Albizu Campos. They waved palm fronds and clapped. Men wearing straw hats carried crosses made of palm leaves. Girls in sundresses threw flowers at the boots of the cadets.

At the last minute, the mayor of Ponce had revoked the parade's permits. He stood in the street to block the demonstration, said it was the governor's orders. A paramilitary police force surrounded the parade and took aim.

The police, armed with 1903 Springfield rifles, Colt .45 automatic pistols, tear gas bombs, and 10-pound Thompson submachine guns, fired into the crowd from all 4 flanks.

The voice over the radio reported at least a dozen deaths and hundreds wounded. An investigation was underway, and Captain Blanco had ordered the arrest of everyone in the vicinity.

Doña Emilia reached out a veined hand and clutched Paula's fingers.

"They were gunned down in cold blood," Paula said. "I don't understand."

Alberto was there. Was he dead? Wounded? Paula felt helpless. She stood to her feet, knocking down the chair under her, eyes full of terror.

Doña Emilia said, *"Tranquila, tranquila, mija. Quédate tranquila."* But how could Paula be calm?

*

The next day, *El Mundo*, one of the island's largest newspapers reported *"Sangre en el suelo,"* blood in the soil. The death toll in Ponce increased to nineteen, but exact names and numbers were uncertain at first. An investigation was underway, and in every café, the bloody exchange between Nationalists and the insular police was hotly debated. Police and English newspapers reported the event as a riot, but witnesses said it was a massacre.

Later that week, Paula held the newspaper with shaking hands and read the names of the dead, which included seventeen men, a woman, and a young girl. Most had been shot in the back as they fled from police. She read and reread the list. No Alberto Ortiz Cruz. Thank God. But if he was not among the dead, then where was he? Among the hundreds who had been wounded? In prison? She prayed a swift prayer. *Dear Jesus, bring him home.*

She brought Alberto's mother, Carmen, the newspaper and read the list of the dead to her. Doña Carmen stood on her small porch breathless as she listened. In her hands, she gripped an iron kettle. After hearing the names, doña Carmen set the kettle down at her feet and wiped her hands on the ragged apron knotted around her waist. "God bless you, mija," she said as she wrapped her twig arms around Paula's neck. Her voice cracked. "All we can do is pray he's not in *La Escuelita.*" La Escualita was what they called the San Juan prison.

Paula imagined Alberto in a windowless cell surrounded by battered cadets. She felt a tightening in her chest.

After gathering branches and dry leaves from under a cooking shed, Rosendo had approached the women on the porch in time to hear Paula read the names. He squatted beside a pile of dry kindling and teepeed the thinnest sticks between four flat stones as he listened. When he spoke, he didn't look up from his work. "Locking the boys up is no good. Nothing but a training ground, if you ask me, for a bunch of boys with big dreams of becoming heroes and martyrs."

Paula's face blanched. "Alberto and the others believe in Albizu Campos, in self-determination."

Rosendo spat in the dirt. "I don't care what he believed. The reality is sugar is at three cents a pound. It takes two in the fields to earn what I used to make in a single day. I told that boy to take on at the Fajardo Sugar hacienda this season. If he'd listened to me, he'd be home."

His mother groaned and put one hand on her lower back. "He helped when he could. God knows we needed the money, but the boy's smart. You know, he read *El Nacionalista* to the *tabaqueros*, and the needle workers requested him by name."

Rosendo softened his tone, but Paula could see the bitterness in his eyes. "You spoiled him, made him soft. At fourteen, I was hulling coffee."

Paula imagined Rosendo as a young man, gripping a large beam like a pestle over his head, cracking the tiny black shells in a giant mortar. She, too, worked in the fields as a young girl. She knew what it was to smash the shells, to throw fistfuls of broken beans, chaff floating in air, caught in a breeze and blowing away, swift as childhood.

"I became a man between two fields, two seasons," Rosendo said, "sugar and coffee. No better than a beast of burden."

Paula had heard men like this her whole life. Men who toiled bent at the waist in the sweltering fields, men who slept in squalid barracks with the other *jornaleros,* landless men migrating from town to town for work. This rhythm, the pendulum swing of the machete, the grinding of beans, beat into the island bones. Rosendo was twenty-four, but when she looked into his eyes, she saw an old man.

"Hell," Carmen interrupted. "I just about forgot to lock them chickens up. Looks like bad weather, too."

"Seems fine to me," Rosendo said.

"Don't you see how them hens are dusting in the sand? Means bad weather every time." His mother shuffled away, coughing wetly and shouting as she went.

Paula watched as Rosendo and his mother scurried around the small front yard with half-hearted energy, herding the three loose hens back into the wooden coop. She then folded the newspaper neatly and tucked it back in her satchel.

She was about to leave when Rosendo returned to the porch. "What else you got there?" He peered into Paula's open satchel, a smile playing in the corner of his mouth.

Paula reached into the bag and handed a pamphlet to Rosendo as he sat on an empty oilcan. "Here, you can keep one," she said. "Alberto used to hand these out to the men in town. It's a call to unite."

Rosendo swatted gnats from his face. "So that's it?" he said. "He left his *mamá* here alone, for this? Let's not forget, he left you behind, too." He lifted the pamphlet as if it were filth. Rosendo looked at the thin paper, the letterpress title. He appeared awkward and self-conscious. He opened it at the crease, running a finger down the smooth, cream paper.

Tentatively, Paula said, "You've got it upside down." With good nature, she repositioned the pamphlet in Rosendo's hands. "There, like that." She encouraged Rosendo to look further, pointing halfway down the page. "It says, 'When tyranny is law, revolution is order.'" She stepped closer to Rosendo, who remained seated, squatted beside him, and continued reading. "We don't have to be doomed to a state of barbarity forever."

"Those are just fancy words," said Rosendo. "Albizu Campos gave a good speech, I'll give him that. But the Yankees locked him up. It's time you people face the facts. It's over."

"Maybe he's in jail, but his voice resounds right here." She tapped the pamphlet in Rosendo's hands, and remembered how

Alberto's eyes glistened when he read her those words for the first time. Reading them now reminded her of his zeal. She longed to connect with him, to share in his struggle.

Paula, full of expectancy, looked up into Rosendo's frowning face. "You want me to read you the rest?"

Rosendo's cheeks flushed. "Don't bother." He crumbled the papers in his fist and shoved the words into the pocket of his slacks. "Let Albizu Campos rot."

A gust of wind rustled the hem of Paula's dress. She tilted her head up to the overcast sky. She sensed the energy in the air shift before she noticed the clouds, heavy and looming. In the near distance, she heard the rumble of thunder.

Rosendo glared at the sky. "I should walk you back home," he said to Paula.

By the time they entered the Fajardo plaza, the shops were closed for the evening. People huddled together under awnings and covered archways. Pearls of rain landed on the palm fronds and bent the stems.

Rosendo placed a firm hand on Paula's shoulder. He directed her through the crowd like a child, maneuvering her away from the plaza center. "We're going to have to make a run for it," he said.

Just then, she saw a white flash followed by a crack of thunder. Paula felt the boom in her chest, and sparks from the electric pole hit the ground at their feet. She placed her hand over her pounding heart and laughed.

Rosendo pulled her by the wrist. "Come on, there's no cover here."

She slipped on the cobblestone, but he steadied her with an arm around her waist. He led her beyond the plaza to where the road gave way to footpaths of muddy earth. He didn't slow down until they were completely out of the township and alone in a clearing surrounded by fields, palms, and lulling cattle.

"This isn't the right way," she said.

"I know a shelter. There's an old barn just beyond this patch."

Lightning illuminated the sky once again. Several seconds later the roar came.

"It'll pass soon," he said. "Come on, you're getting soaked."

"I should go home." She knew the risk of being spotted alone with him. The town chatter was enough to make her hesitate, but there was something more, an instinct like an alarm warning her to turn back.

"Don't be stupid. This is closer. You can't outrun a storm."

The rain poured down, muddying her shoes as she considered her options. Sprint back to the plaza and look like a scared fool, offend Rosendo, or prove to this man and to herself that she, too, could be courageous, as spirited as the girls who'd joined the Palm Sunday parade in Ponce. He was Alberto's older brother, after all. She yielded to his confidence and reluctantly followed him.

The curing barn was abandoned and sticky with heat. The smell of tobacco clung to the walls, a bitter, masculine smell that reminded her of the earth and burning wood. Bundles of leaves strung on wooden sticks hung overhead from the rafters. Rosendo held a brittle tobacco bundle back with one arm. Paula ducked her head and passed under his arm and into a small space between the rows.

"Keep an eye out for black snakes," he said.

She looked at her feet, wide-eyed. The log walls were chinked with clay. It was dim.

"Maybe we shouldn't be here," she said.

"It's fine." He sat on the packed dirt and patted the spot beside him.

"No, thank you. I'd rather stand."

"Suit yourself."

The rain rattled against the rooftop. Paula wrapped bare arms around her soaked, muddy dress.

Rosendo laughed at her. "You look like a drenched rat."

She grimaced. "Luz Marí is gonna kill me."

He stretched out like a contented cat. "Nothing you can't scrub out. It's still coming down pretty hard."

"It's my best dress," she said. "Otherwise, I wouldn't mind so much." Paula examined the ground carefully before sitting. "I don't mind rain." She sat and adjusted the hem of her dress to cover her legs.

The ground vibrated with a thunderous clap, and she clasped her hands into tight fists near her mouth.

"You're so jumpy," he said.

"It's hot in here." She looked at him and noticed a drop of rainwater slip from the hair at his temples and travel down his neck. Or was it sweat? She felt nervous, and her eyes darted about the ground and then overhead at the network of beams.

"During curing, it's like an oven. Hot as hell," he said. "But this place has been let go for years."

"How do you know?"

"Just look at that roof." A corner of the gabled roof sagged.

"Is it safe?"

"You worry too much."

"What about the snakes?"

"I was teasing," he said with a sigh. "The rain will pass soon, but we shouldn't be out in that lightning. It's the lightning that kills a man. Not snakes. A storm caught a bunch of us field hands knee-deep in sugar once, and before I knew it, the man beside me was struck dead." He snapped his fingers. "Just like that."

"How awful."

Rosendo shrugged and leaned back on his hands.

"Why'd you come back here?"

"To Fajardo?" he asked. "You want the real reason?"

"Yes."

"I spent years working at a hacienda, but lost my place."

"I know, but why?"

"Fighting. A bunch of us workers went on strike because the union leaders and the landowner cheated us out of what we had coming. A few men mouthed off, I threw a rock. Things got out of hand, and in the end, my name ended up on somebody's shit list. Went to prison for three months after that. I can't go back."

"That's the kind of thing Alberto always talked about. He said the workers needed to unite, fight back the way they did in Bombay or Dublin."

"He doesn't know anything about it. I couldn't tell you about them other places, but here, no amount of flag waving is gonna change a damn thing."

"They weren't just waving flags," she said, indignant. "They were raising an army, *cadets de la República*."

"Don't you get it? It's over. Albizu Campos is doing ten years in a federal prison. Is that what you want? For Alberto to join him behind bars? Because that's exactly where he's headed."

"No, of course not." She shook her head. "But he's not like you."

"What's that supposed to mean?"

"I don't know. It's like Albizu Campos said, sacrifice for a sacred cause. He believes that."

Rosendo widened his eyes. "Even if it means violence?"

Paula shook her head and looked down at her muddy shoes. "He believes in justice, not violence."

"Can you even have one without the other?"

"I don't know," she said. "Ever since he left, I've had this awful feeling in the pit of my stomach. I don't think he's coming back." Her voiced cracked.

"What do you mean?"

"It's just a feeling. He'd never be a sugar slave," she said. "He couldn't stand a *mayordomo* riding down his back for the rest of his life. Maybe they're not cracking whips, but it's slavery all the same."

A flutter of panic turned her stomach. To defend Alberto's dream was to let her own dreams of their life together drift away on an unyielding current. Dread and disappointment surged inside her, but she did her best to shove down the sting and surrender to it. She arched her back to stretch, to catch her breath. "Can we talk about something else?"

Rosendo watched her with a steady expression, then said, "You hear that thunder? When I was a boy, they said that the sound of thunder was the god of lightning."

"Who told you that?"

"Elba, the woman who raised me."

"I thought you didn't believe in those things."

He ignored her and continued. "Thousands of years ago, in the second heaven, Changó stole his favorite bride Oyá from his half-brother Ogún. She, too, was a fierce warrior, a sensual lover. She dressed in orange, like you, that day we first met. She was his ancient tornado bride, sexy and mysterious."

"Those are just folktales."

"Maybe. Just because something's an old story, don't mean it's not true. All I know is Changó can mount a man like a horse. I've seen it, felt it. As real as lightning."

"That's all idolatry. Nothing more than superstitions." Paula wrung out the folds of her dress.

"People petition the Catholic saints, don't they? What's the difference?"

"The saints were real people."

"Real? What's real?" Rosendo inched closer. "Aren't our ancestors as real as any man's?"

She shrugged. "How would I know? I'm Adventist. We've got one mediator alone, and that's Jesus."

He snickered. "Always preaching."

"I don't get you. You learned all this from Elba, right? But I thought you ran away from that life."

"You can't outrun the stories that make you. Shit, words take root, like seeds."

His tone frightened her more than his irritation. She wanted to back away, but the wall hemmed her in.

"But what if they were lies?"

"No matter. It's all lies we tell ourselves to get to the truth of things."

"Maybe," she said.

"Maybe we're not that different," he said. "Maybe there are forces we can't see, stories playing themselves out over and over again. I know you don't see it, but I've got convictions. I might not be a disciple like my baby brother, and I'm certainly no nun, like you. Or are you the martyr? I've not made up my mind yet."

"What if I'm neither of those things?"

"I like surprises." He dragged his thumb down Paula's cheek.

"Please don't." She pushed his hand away. She could run, but he'd outrun her. Her throat went dry.

"There's some mud," he said, stroking her face again.

"I can get it myself." She hastily wiped at her cheek with the back of her hand.

"You don't have to be afraid of me," he said. "I'm not going to hurt you."

"I'm not afraid," she said, but she could hear the thick terror in her voice. He could hear it, too.

"Why don't you ever look at me?" he asked.

"What?"

"Why do you always look away from me?"

She stared firmly ahead as she said, "I don't."

He gripped her chin between his thumb and forefinger and forced her head up to face him. "I like to look at you."

She lifted her eyes to his, large, frightened tears blurring her vision. "Please, don't." She jerked her neck, pulling away from him, but he gripped at her jaw harder, so hard she could feel back teeth dig into the inside of one cheek.

A tear slipped down her face.

"You look at me like I'm a rabid dog," he said. "I won't bite." With his knuckle, he traced the tear as it slipped down to her neck.

"Don't," she said.

"Don't what? Don't think about you? Don't touch you?"

She squirmed, but he pinned her wrists over her head, the weight of his body crushing her. "No." She couldn't move.

His hands reached down the front of her dress and groped her breasts. "Don't move."

"Stop." Her voice caught in her chest, shaky, so low it sounded almost inaudible. Then again, louder, "Don't."

"Quiet."

He was a towering shadow above her, grabbing at the soaked fabric of her dress. He tugged, almost tearing the neckline.

She felt the strain of the fabric, heard the snap of pulled threads. "Wait," she said, breathless. In panic, she said, "Don't rip it."

"What?"

"I'll take it off." She looked directly into his face. "Please, don't rip it." The cotton was thin, delicate. How could she explain it being torn? To explain the dress to her sister-in-law would mean to explain everything, every humiliation. Every wrong decision. No matter what happened next, she would be to blame, that much she knew. With trembling hands, she began unbuttoning from her neck to her waist. He watched as she slid out of the damp dress and folded it neatly beside her.

When he spoke into her neck, his voice was cracked, strained. "Be still," he said softly, digging fingers into her skin, prying her legs apart. "Relax."

After, she lay curled in a ball, shivering in the dirt, a trickle of blood between her legs. He stood above her, buttoning his pants. He felt his pocket for a handkerchief, and remembered Alberto's liberty pamphlets there. He flung it at her. "Don't act so innocent. Clean yourself up. I'll take you home."

Paula's upbringing taught her to seal her suffering to the cross. But how? Her mind raced, and she saw again Rosendo's face shifting in shadow, the fury in his pale eyes, raging hunger one moment, cold contempt the next. She felt the pain, the shame, and the sickening wet of Rosendo dripping out from between her legs. She felt the sting of mortification and the needle pricks of disgrace. Then she heaved and vomited into mud.

Paula stumbled home, blaming herself, drenched and shaking. She said the rains overtook her on the road. Said she'd slipped, soaking her only shoes. Tears streaked her face, but in silence, she bore her sister-in-law's scolding. Luz Marí complained that even an *idiota* knew better than to run in the rain, unless she wanted to catch her death. She demanded that she scrub every inch of the dress. Paula hefted the wash pail onto her hip and walked out the door, away from the irritated cluck of Luz Marí and the gawking eyes of her nieces and nephews.

At the water spigot behind the house, she scoured her face, neck, and between her thighs. As she rubbed at the stains on the fabric, she heard her brother's heavy boots slosh toward the house. The yelp of a neighboring dog, the clank of the iron gate. From behind the house, she could clearly hear the agitated shrill of his wife's voice, relaying the story of his good-for-nothing sister and the soaking wet dress.

When her brother dismissed his wife's complaints, Paula felt relieved. She gave up scouring the brown splotches on the fabric, thinking it better to let the clothes sit in bleach and water overnight. She changed into a plain cotton housedress and reentered the home. She didn't feel like talking, so her sister-in-law's cold shoulder did not have its intended effect. Instead, the two women prepared the evening meal, standing shoulder to shoulder, neither saying a word. Paula lost herself in thought: Rosendo's clawing hands, the pounding rain, her own voice pleading, *You're hurting me.* She was shaking, blind to her surroundings, until she grabbed the handle of the tin pot with her bare hands and scalded herself.

"What's the matter with you?" her sister-in-law said. "You're useless tonight."

"I'm sorry." Paula blew on her fingers and thumbed the red patch of skin into the cave of her fist.

"Stick it in the water pail," said Luz Marí. "Go on. Hurry up."

Fresh tears filled Paula's eyes, but she barely felt the burn.

RED DEVILS

City Island, NY
1982

Esther sat at the kitchen table counting the little blue pills her dad Jude called Blue Angels and the tiny red pills he called Red Devils. First, she sorted the pills by color into two piles, then she counted, moving her lips as she spoke the numbers under her breath: forty-five, forty-six, forty-seven. Each time she whispered a number, she scooted a pill aside with her pointer finger, careful not to lose count.

She knew her dad never used the pills he pocketed from the pharmacies where he worked. He didn't have a drug habit to feed. He'd never swallowed even a single aspirin in his whole life, and that was the God's honest truth.

Her father worked eighty hours a week between two hospitals in the city. He worked overtime and holidays.

"I've never been sick a day in my life," her dad said, pride in his voice. "Didn't even take off for my old man's funeral." He'd also missed her birth, missed holidays, missed recitals. So when he asked her to count the Blue Angels and the Red Devils, she did it gladly, just to be near him.

If you asked him, he probably couldn't tell you exactly why he had started stealing the pills. He took them because he could. It was easy. So easy, he considered it plain stupid not to take them. Any right-minded opportunist in New York City would have done

81

the same. You could make a killing selling meds on the side, and her dad knew plenty of guys eager to pay cash per pill.

Maybe he didn't need a reason. He'd spent his young life idolizing the toughs from the old neighborhood in Brooklyn. Maybe he couldn't help himself. Like the time she'd watched him steal electric tape from the hardware store or tube socks from Woolworth's.

Not too long ago, she'd watched two Sears security guards tackle her dad at the store exit. They pinned him to the ground and pulled a fistful of drill bits out of the inner pocket of his leather vest. With his hands cuffed behind his back, lying on his belly, he looked up at her and said, "I did this to teach you a lesson."

It was no secret that her dad hated the hospitals where he worked, hated the pharmaceutical industry, the good-for-nothing doctors, sickness, and sick people. He hated the Clorox smell of death, the fluorescent overhead lights, the claustrophobic walls, the pissed-off nurses, the hellish commute, and the unshakeable feeling that everything around him was going to shit.

"We're sticking it to the man," he told her as she sorted neat blue and red piles. She nodded and smiled, giving him a thumbs up like the Fonz. She didn't know who *the man* was, but that didn't matter. Stealing the pills made her dad spark with life. It made his job and marriage somehow easier to stomach, and he said it meant he could retire in less than ten years.

Esther didn't understand anything about being a father, but she did know what it felt like to be in relationship with her mother—powerless. Maybe that was enough to spark her father's minor rebellions, the tit for tat dynamic that persisted until his death.

If truth be told, his morale was low, and he'd unconditionally surrendered to her mother's will the fall before Esther's birth. Maybe it was the pregnancy, but her mother never did get used to living aboard her father's boat like she'd envisioned. She didn't like the shifting ground below her feet, the way the early morning wakes smashed into the craft, or the ceaseless rocking. She didn't like the way her hands felt numb with cold, the smell of salt and fish that made her nose run, or the slippery, icy pier, which she insisted was one hazardous misstep away from a fall and potential miscarriage.

Her mother had tried her best to convince her father that they'd be better off in a house, something in the suburbs with a yard, a nursery, a garage for his motorcycle and tools, but he huffed at the thought of living "on land." *The Lady Viking* was family, and he wouldn't discuss it.

No matter how often her mother scrubbed with bleach, she said the sheets, carpet, and even her own skin smelled of mold. She complained, but he would hear none of it. His body seemed impenetrable to the cold, and he could sit for hours watching the rain bounce off water. To him, it was enough to sit on a deck chair and flip through *Hot Rod* magazine or have his hooks on the bottom after catfish.

He knew she had a temper, but he hadn't expected her to grab a ten-gallon gas drum and begin to pour. He didn't understand the tempestuous nature cloaked under her mother's skin. He was at work at the time, so she started in the galley. Poured gas over the table. Tipped the drum over the propane tank used for grilling. With both arms in a swinging motion, she propelled gas up and out onto the varnished cabinets. Liquid leaked over the stove and the dinette, and sloshed onto the single-panel curtains above the small sink. In the master's cabin she doused unmade sheets, poured gas over pillows.

From her purse, she pulled out a worn matchbook, struck a slender match, and watched the flame ignite. As soon as she threw the match, she ran. The fifty-seven-foot, Chris-Craft Catalina with its twin engines held five hundred gallons of diesel. Burning tracks climbed up the galley walls and spread to the cabins. The flames surged over the vinyl ceiling liner and onto the beds. Outside, combustion followed the wind, igniting the fiberglass deck like kindling. Smoke and light purged every surface. As the sun began to set over the Hudson River, smoke lifted a dragon tail cloud.

Residents at the marina set the flaring boat adrift, loose from the pilings, before the powerful flames could spread like a pestilence onto the other boats. The water was aglow with the flashing lights of fire trucks and police cars. By the time Esther's father returned from work to the marina, all that remained of *The Lady Viking* was sinking rubble and ribbons of black smoke.

The story of her mother burning the boat became family legend, and in the end, her father agreed to a waterfront house in City Island, New York.

To avoid rush hour traffic, her dad switched to working nights or left the house no later than dawn. In brutal weather, he took the Jeep and fell asleep on more than one occasion behind the wheel, landing in a ditch the first time and entirely flipping the car the second. He walked away from the accidents miraculously uninjured. After he almost totaled the Jeep, he started taking the Harley into work. On the bike, he said he felt more alive, more awake. He said it was the only time of the day when both his hands and his feet knew exactly what to do.

Sometimes he'd take her for a spin. She'd wrap her arms around his stomach, and he'd work the brakes, gears, and clutch masterfully. Sometimes, she felt as if the bike was an extension of his body. She liked leaning into curves, finding the perfect balance as the road dipped beneath them. She liked the taste of salt air, the rushing drop of temperature that always happened as they neared the water. She liked the smooth hum of motor, metal, and pavement. The adrenaline of rain. The way time expanded as he crossed the City Island Bridge or hugged the coast along the East River.

"Ride's over," he'd say, and sit idle until she jumped off the bike, careful not to burn her shin on the exhaust pipe.

Once, after one of their rides, he squinted down at her from his bike and said, "It's like, when I switch off the engine, nothing makes sense."

There was something lost and bitter in his tone, and she wished she could sort him out with the same ease she sorted devils from angels.

*

Esther didn't remember cracking her head into the front windshield, but she recalled the rush hour traffic that preceded it, the way she sat on her knees unbuckled in the front seat. She and her dad had been on the Throgs Neck Bridge when he'd fallen asleep behind the wheel and rear-ended a car. Back home, as her mom picked the broken glass from Esther's hair, she said he couldn't be trusted, not behind the wheel or anywhere else for that matter. She called him a liar, a cheat, a thief, and worse.

Had it been just the one accident, maybe Esther would have let it slide, but there'd been others: the time when she was four, when she had stood behind him while he hammered into wood and caught the upswing of the hammer right over her eyebrow. Or the time she chased him down a mountain path in Arizona and fell hard into a cactus. She counted the scars she'd collected over the years, but it wasn't until their vacation in Daytona Beach that she decided, once and for all, that her mother had been right about him all along.

It was early April, and the Atlantic Ocean had felt unseasonably warm. Her father gripped her wrist and lifted her body high above the white foam of the waves. In the near distance, a flock of surfers floated, catching offshore breaks. She and her father watched the water swell, taking their cues from the surfers who paddled toward monster crests.

"Get ready," he shouted. Her stomach tightened, and her wide eyes watched the surge barrel towards them. "Jump!" He yanked her skyward.

She sprang over the rolling wave, laughing as his bicep lifted her feet. Then the water drifted out to sea with the current tugging at her calves and thighs. He held on tight to her wrist, anchoring her against the receding water.

Behind them stretched a line of high-rise hotels and condos. Volkswagens, hot rods, Jeeps, vans, and motorcycles parked on every inch of sand. Her mother sat reading a paperback under a beach umbrella.

Esther looked back and saw her mother cup her mouth and shout in their direction. Above the pounding of the breaks, the music and the wind, her mother's voice was only a vague murmur.

"What did she say?" Spray hit Esther's face as she spoke, and she tasted salt.

"Beats me." Her father stood in a swash of backwater.

A few feet away, what looked like a glistening, glass-blown sculpture drifted on a current. "What's that?" Esther said.

Her father released his grip on her wrist. "I don't know. A balloon, maybe? Check it out."

Esther bobbed closer and could see that the blue and violet glass wasn't glass at all. It was gelatinous. A kidney-shaped mold of floating Jell-O. Polished blue agate, clear as crystal quartz. She reached her hand out toward the wavy reflections of light and touched. A jolt of excruciating pain shot up her arm. Electric, paralyzing pain. Screaming.

*

Once, when she'd asked her father about the green tattooed heart on his bicep, he rolled up his T-shirt sleeve to give her a better look. "This was my first tattoo," he said. It was several inches wide, and a black banner filled the center of the heart.

Esther traced the inked line with her finger. "What's that?"

He shrugged and let the sleeve fall loose. "It used to be a name," he said. "But your mother gave me hell, so I had it inked over."

"Whose name?"

"Donald Duck," he said.

She smirked.

"You know your mother," he said. "She's the jealous type."

"Jealous of a cartoon? Come on," Esther said. "That's not true. Whose name was it?"

He gestured to her with his thumb. "Can't pull anything over on this one," he said to the empty air. "If you must know, it was Adrienne. Adrienne's name."

Esther had never met his first wife, but she heard her mother call the woman crazy. A psycho.

"We were just a couple of kids back then," her father said. "She used to hop on the back of my motorcycle, and we'd take off to Coney Island."

Her father said he'd saved summer money from stocking grocery shelves to buy his first motorcycle.

"Was it a Harley?" she'd asked.

"No, a Triumph. A bargain for only two hundred and fifty bucks."

He told her Adrienne used to say he looked like Marlon Brando from *The Wild One*.

Esther had never seen the movie, but she imagined a thinner, younger dad riding his motorcycle to Coney Island. She imagined snake charmers and fire-eaters, a Ferris wheel, and cotton candy.

When she asked him about Coney Island, he said, "Back then, you could watch freak shows for a nickel." He and Adrienne spent all their time making out in the Tunnel of Love, eating pizza slices on the boardwalk, and riding the Cyclone.

Esther tried to picture it in her mind. She imagined her father as Popeye walking alongside Olive Oyl.

Her father pulled a toothpick out of his front pocket and wiggled it between his molars. "In those days, mostly greasers or guys in the Navy got tattoos."

"But you weren't in the Navy," she said.

"I know. Maybe I wanted to prove I was as good as those toughs."

When she asked him more about Adrienne, he said, "Anyone ever tell you children should be seen and not heard?"

"Come on," she'd insisted. "You haven't even told me what happened to her. Did she like your tattoo?"

"How the hell should I know?"

"Well, didn't she say anything about it?"

"Not really. But the day after I got it, she left me a note on my bike. It said, *Roses are red with lots of charm. Don't let your mother see your right arm.* She was funny like that. Clever."

"Did your mom get mad?"

"She hit the roof," he said, "but it made no difference. Adrienne and I got married a few months later. But that was a long time ago. Old history."

For Esther, Adrienne was a curiosity, just another nickel freak from her father's past, as imaginary as a cartoon character. Nothing remained of her except an inky black smudge, a banner of black ink on her father's arm.

"What happened to her?" Esther asked.

Her dad scratched his neck. "She got sick."

"Sick how?"

"Adrienne stopped eating. She got down to ninety-five pounds. Maybe less. She got to stashing bottles of iodine in her purse."

"What for?"

"Hell if I know," he said. "I was in pharmacy college back then, holding down two jobs. Every little thing set that woman off."

"Mom says Adrienne was a nut job."

Her father rolled his eyes. "Look, do us both a favor, and don't believe everything your mother tells you, all right?"

"But Mom says she went to the loony bin."

Her father sighed. "I took her to Hillside Hospital for a few weeks. Back then, the doctors used to do something called insulin shock therapy. Morons. I took her in for depression, and they shot her up with a needle full of insulin."

"Why?" Esther knew about insulin. Her favorite aunt, Rosa, had diabetes, and had gone blind from the disease.

"The doctors didn't know any better back then. They never do," he said.

"So she didn't get better?"

"No," he said. "She got worse. She went into a coma for thirty minutes, and woke up worse off than when she'd gone in."

"What did you do?"

"I split."

*

From below the water's surface, long tendrils stung across Esther's back, her arms, her neck. Blue pearls of pain. Fiery tentacles tangled and knotted in her hair.

Her father pulled at the Portuguese man-of-war, ripping away at the stringy fire. "Jesus Christ," he said over and over, his own hands burning with every touch.

Her chest tightened. She couldn't breathe. Someone ran towards them. Her mother? A lifeguard? "She's going into shock," a voice said.

Her father lifted her into his arms. "Call 911."

"Her lips are blue," her mother's voice screamed. "What the hell is it? Her lips are turning blue. She can't breathe."

"Anaphylaxis," her father said, as he ran towards the shore.

"What?" her mother shouted at his back.

"She's allergic."

*

In her nightmares, Esther dreamed she'd been rushed to the hospital and dressed in a long cotton smock that fell to her knees. A pale nurse placed her in a metal bed with side rails. A doctor in a starched white coat walked between the beds, injecting faceless girls with long needles of insulin. When he turned Esther onto her stomach, she tried to scream but couldn't make a sound.

"Why would Dad tell me to touch it?" Esther studied her reflection in the hotel mirror.

Her mother kneeled beside her and rubbed hydrocortisone cream on Esther's swollen arms. "Because he's an idiot."

For weeks, her mother berated him. She criticized and rebuked his carelessness, and Esther was left with the pervasive imprint of his negligence.

In time, Esther wondered if he had even told her to touch the man-of-war on purpose as a cruel joke. In her mind, her father became a man of shifting sands, unsafe.

She remembered nothing about the hospital, where she'd been given a shot of epinephrine. Her swollen lips and tongue returned to normal, and all that remained were the red welts on her skin. Those lasted for weeks.

Her mother said, "You look like someone whipped the crap out of you."

Her father had the same welts on his hands. He had ripped the Portuguese man-of-war off her body. Under the surface of the water, its tendrils had extended for at least thirty feet.

Still, her mother blamed him, and Esther, too, learned that on the surface, nothing could be trusted, especially not fathers.

What was a handful of pills, anyway? What was ten to twenty pills a day, two hospitals, eighty hours a week? In one year alone, he'd probably taken more than eight thousand pills, but only she was counting.

CUERO Y SANGRE

City Island, New York
1980

While Jude worked between two hospitals and Esther went to kindergarten, Isabel chanted and called on her *orishas*. She made special gifts for Yemayá, and Yemayá became her intimate guardian. With her madrina, she walked the woods, listening for the voices of spirits, and she devoted more and more of her time to trying to open her ears to the sounds beyond sound.

Initially, after Esther's birth, Paula moved in to help with the baby. Isabel carefully hid her statues, beads, spells, and charms from her mother, but in less than a week Paula said, "You keep that voodoo *porquería* out of my sight or I'm leaving."

Despite Paula's objections, she didn't leave. She griped and complained, but never packed her bags. Her complete devotion to her newborn granddaughter kept her anchored to the City Island house. She rocked the baby to sleep, woke to feed her in the middle of the night, changed her diapers, anointed her bedroom door with olive oil, and rebuked Isabel's spirits in the name of Jesus.

Isabel gave Paula the bedroom and bathroom on the first floor, and there she lived for the first seven years of Esther's life, raising the girl like a second mother.

*

Lourdes said if Isabel learned to listen, the spirits would tell her which trees and herbs would help her cause. Isabel's ear attuned to the voices of spirits, like tuning a radio to a primordial station. The world opened up, far stranger and far more mysterious than she'd ever known it to be.

Having grown up in the projects, surrounded by filth and crumbling concrete, walking alone in the woods held its own small terrors. At first, her mind spiraled with frightened thoughts of psycho killers and rapist perverts hiding behind every bush. She couldn't relinquish the sense that behind every tree lurked unforeseeable horrors. Her eyes darted down deserted paths, waiting for muggers and leather-faced chainsaw hackers.

In time, she learned to relax, to quiet her inner terror, and listen. Isabel steadied her breath and focused on her chanting. She learned that everything in nature had *ashé*, life force, and tapping into this energy was her life path. She imagined herself linked somehow to her native Taíno and Yoruba ancestors, communing with the natural world, where herbs, birds, and trees poured forth speech. Here, among nature, was a wellspring of ancient voices waiting to be heard.

At first, Isabel heard only vague murmurings. In time, she hoped the murmurings would sharpen into words, and she knew she was on the path to seeing her invisible spiritual guides face to face. The swish of dry leaves in the breeze rustled with energy. Light sparkling off a stream trickled whispers, and the more she listened and practiced, the more she understood. For the first time, she felt connected to something larger than herself.

She had become a full member of the Santeria spiritual community in the Bronx. There were no rosters, no membership cards. This was a clandestine, secret community, a family that transformed their jewel-box living rooms into festive drum circles, gatherings devoted to dancing, offerings of flowers, fruit, and blood. Rooms glowed with the warm light of votive candles, smelled of incense, coconut, and cigars, and pulsed with joyous, primal rhythms. The city fell away, and Isabel was transported across seas, tucked under the canopy of wild terrain. This was a nowhere land without boundaries or limitations. Her new brothers and sisters devoted their afternoons to the exploration of spiritual forces. They gathered to invoke the spirits' prescriptions to heal sick family members, to return ex-lovers, and to free desperate sons and daughters from prison.

Over time, Isabel felt her psychic strength increase. During her walks in Pelham Park, the voices from the trees and foliage spoke to her with clarity. Her dreams took on new life, filled with symbolic imagery waiting to be interpreted. From her waterfront backyard in City Island, she walked out into the Long Island Sound up to her waist, carrying pennies and white roses as gifts for Yemayá, and she felt pure delight on the nights she felt Yemayá rock her and sing her to sleep. Signs called *odu* abounded in the flight of birds or in a pattern in the clouds. She felt elated to be privy to secrets, to feel the world crack open.

As her devotion to the *orishas* grew, Jude relinquished more and more into her hands. He gave Isabel complete control of the household decisions.

The next step in Isabel's practice was a secret ceremony called the *Asiento*, which would make her a *Santera*, a priestess. She would have to submit and become the literal seat of her *orisha*, possession. The crown of her head, called *Ori*, her seat of consciousness, would become one with her *orisha*. Her godparents said it was like being mounted, but the horse image only made her feel worse. She'd heard that sometimes the mounted person could be endangered or erupt in violent outbursts, and the idea of complete possession terrified her. She'd seen the agonized looks of terror fill the men and women right before they were replaced by the spirit. To be possessed was to be cast out of the vessel that is flesh with an explosion of self transcending upward and out to nothingness, a vacuum and void so deep that she shuddered to think of it. But possession was part of the path; it was expected, demanded.

At the last drumming ceremony, she'd felt as if someone had pulled back the veil dividing the city from an ancient dream.

Hourglass *batá* drums rested in the laps of three male drummers dressed head to toe in white. They pounded the *toque*, a beat to call the *orishas*. With the palms of their hands slapping both ends of the drums, the men's complex rhythm pulsed through the living room of the Bronx apartment and spilled out into the kitchen, where more people pressed together to listen.

Isabel had felt the music in her chest, but Ernesto said the drums weren't even sacred. He frowned and crossed his arms. "Totally unacceptable," he said. "Unconsecrated drums."

Recently, Ernesto had been complaining more and more how newcomers were mishandling their traditions. "Traditions are strictly obeyed in Cuba," he said. "Not like here, where anything goes."

For months, Ernesto had been drilling into Isabel the importance of authenticity during ceremonies. "If you want to make saint," he said, "we must go to the source. We must go to Cuba. That's where you go. Not here, where they initiate two-punk gangbangers or any old asshole off the streets."

Isabel smiled weakly, but her muscles tightened. She was tired of being prodded. Of all places, why Cuba? "I've heard of plenty of *Asientos* right here in New York," she said. Ernesto had godchildren all over the city, in Miami, even Los Angeles. It didn't seem fair that he insist she travel to Cuba.

Ernesto scowled. "It's your own fault for dragging your feet this long. You can't say I didn't warn you from the start. This is no game you're playing."

"I know." She nodded. "Offending the *orishas* means trouble." Her words came out snarkily, but she didn't care. She imagined her *Egun* ancestors, irritated and chiming in, "You're lucky you haven't gotten into an accident by now. Sooner or later, if you don't straighten up, you're gonna find yourself wrapped around a tree." Isabel bit her lower lip in frustration.

Lourdes agreed with Ernesto. "You're pressing your luck," she said. Her concerned expression darkened. Now she seemed irritated. "Stubbornness threatens not only yourself, but everyone around you. You need to prove your devotion. You can't go around delaying your *Asiento* forever."

There was no going back, only going forward, toward sacrifice and obedience. Isabel had known that from the beginning.

Ernesto softened his tone. "It's up to you, mija. Heavenly rage is nothing to screw around with. Think about your daughter." Their prodding reminded her of the fire-and-brimstone messages taught to her as a child. Was there no escape from a world of angry gods?

Ernesto and Lourdes walked closer to the drummers, leaving Isabel to her thoughts. She had less seniority, and so she stood on the outskirts of the crowd. The mother drum, the *Iya*, called to the other two smaller drums, and the beat accelerated. From the center of the crowd, the master of ceremonies, the *oriaté*, dressed in red for the spirit Changó. He sang in the Yoruba language and leapt about the room to the beat. With wild eyes, he reached out into the crowd, laying hands on the heads of men and women around him. Everyone watched in agonized anticipation. When he touched a woman beside Isabel, she whirlpooled her body, spinning and spinning without end. Another dropped to the ground. Men went limp, scarecrow legs and arms jerking instinctually to the *bata bata bata* of the drums. One by one, contagious energy ignited the dancers.

Before Isabel felt the touch upon her own head, she saw the piercing eyes of Changó. She felt the muscles in her legs jolt with a visceral force, spinning her like a top. A primal charge compelled her across the floor. A spiritual current twirled her until the walls all around fell away. The floor was no longer under her feet, nor the dirt beneath the floors, nor her feet beneath her body. Time vibrated, shifted, and scattered. Only the drums remained. Only the incessant spinning, and the *whip whip whip* of wind.

Six hours later, she collapsed to the ground.

In the morning, she had no memory of the drum ceremony. From the moment Changó set hands on her, she crossed the thin boundary of awareness. With no inkling of her dancing, no hangover from the endless bottles of dry white wine, no soreness in her muscles, she wondered if the possession had happened at all. The night was lost to her. Her fugitive memory had escaped, and for the night, she had detached from time itself.

Being out of control frightened her more than she was willing to admit to her godparents. She didn't like the idea of invading spirits coming and going into her body as they pleased. Lourdes assured her that the *Asiento* was a means to control. The way to power. Isabel felt uncertain. Could she really placate these spirits for the rest of her life?

Ernesto was unwavering. "You need *Asiento* to strengthen your control over the *orishas*. Otherwise, you're open game for ambush." Again, he emphasized the importance to going back to the origin, of seeking authentic practice. Each time she refused, she saw the disappointment and frustration in his face. Veneration no longer seemed a choice when the alternative was unspeakable doom. Could the oracles trap her in an endless cycle?

She believed he was being unreasonable. *Asiento* was hard enough, but traveling to Cuba was absurd. In exasperation, she said, "If authenticity is such a big deal, wouldn't going back to Nigeria make more sense?" As soon as she said the heated words, she regretted it. She knew better than to argue with her elder, but it was too late. There were factions in the community that pitted the African ways against the Cuban traditions, and the subject had become political. The damage was done. The words and the tone in which they were said tainted the air between them.

His eyes were furious. "I'm tired of debating this with you," he said. "It's in Cuba, not the homeland, where our rituals are best preserved." He clicked his tongue. "You're obviously not ready. This is your spiritual future, not mine."

"I'm not ready," she admitted to her madrina later, and she did everything she could to resist. She made excuses and delayed the ceremony.

Her mother spoke of dying to herself and being born again in Jesus, and Lourdes used the same language to describe the rebirth and resurrection of a new consciousness in the *orishas*. Her mother demonized the practice, called it witchcraft.

Isabel didn't know what to make of it all. The metaphors of birth, death, and new life were the same, but Jesus had spent half his time casting demonic spirits out of people, freeing them of possession. When she tried to imagine the *Asiento*, shivers ran up her arms. She didn't like the feeling that night at the drum circle. Losing control, being powerless to become powerful. It felt counter intuitive. Once, she tried to bring up her questions with her mother, but Paula declared the *orishas* demons, counterfeit spirits, and it turned into an ugly argument.

Isabel wasn't convinced. She needed more time to think, to figure it out herself, but her time was running short. If her guiding *orishas* gave up on her, she would be left alone, vulnerable to unnamable evils. She knew the punishment for disobedience was severe, but she saw no clear way: apostasy from her spiritual community and curses for disobedience, or estrangement from her mother. "If you become a Santera, I am not stepping foot inside your house," her mother had warned, and Isabel knew she would keep her word.

She needed a third option.

There was one other reason for postponing this next step. The financial cost alone would be astronomical. Madrina had said it would cost at least five thousand dollars, and require an extensive amount of time away from home, seven days. She would have to shave her hair and dress in white for an entire year. She would not be permitted to wear makeup, nail polish, or any jewelry apart from the sacred jewelry permitted by the *orishas*. For a full year, there would be no way to hide her practice from family or friends. How could she explain it to her neighbors on City Island, to Esther's teachers in Larchmont? Everyone would know. She imagined herself shaved bald and dressed in all white on the sidelines of soccer games, at ballet recitals, at lunches at the yacht club. Impossible. They'd think she'd joined a cult or lost her mind. This ancient practice, hidden in a concrete jungle of the city where people could remain anonymous, felt more exposed among nosey neighbors in the suburbs.

"Just a little more time," Isabel prayed. "I promise, I will devote my whole life to the *orishas*. Just give me more time." But Lourdes said her time had run out. She said Isabel was neglecting the will of her *Egun*, and treading on dangerous ground.

*

A small gathering congregated in Lourdes' basement for an intercessory *misa*. Several men and women sat in a semicircle at one end of the dining room table. Isabel could read in the expressions of the others, a mix of sympathy and condemnation. Ignoring the *Egun* reflected poorly on their madrina, perhaps implicating their whole *casa de santos*.

White linen covered a table, and upon the fabric, Lourdes placed a vase filled with white carnations and several clear glasses of water. Two white candles framed a brass handbell, and a silver crucifix rested inside the largest glass of water to represent the crossroads between the living and the dead.

"I'm sorry, Madrina," said Isabel. She felt embarrassed to be reprimanded in front of the other godchildren. On City Island, she hid her ancestral shrine on a shelf in her bedroom closet behind a pair of red, knee-high leather boots. There she placed the stemmed glasses of water, the white candles, the caramel candies and cigars the spirit of her papi Rosendo always favored. Each time she tried to honor him, she struggled to practice the *bóveda*. She could make it through the Our Father, say the Hail Marys and the Glory Be, but when it came to praying directly to her papi to intercede on her behalf, she couldn't find the words. Deep down, she had not forgiven him, didn't trust him.

She thought of the time she'd failed the first grade, and he'd held her by her ankles outside their fourth-floor window. The Christmas he'd shoved her so hard her panty-hosed feet slipped on the kitchen linoleum, and she fell. She'd been nineteen, and that Christmas, her father sang a heartfelt "Dulce Consuelo" to the tune of "Blessed Assurance" and preached from Lamentations.

That night the Holy Spirit poured out, filling the church with such voltage that some said they smelled smoke.

Lourdes motioned Isabel to step forward with her hand. Isabel said, "I didn't mean to be neglectful," remembering how the water in the stemmed glasses grew musty in her closet, how the flower petals dried and shriveled. She tried to sound repentant, but instead, the words came out defensive.

"Don't say sorry to me," Lourdes said. "Apologize to your blood ancestors. They're waiting for you to honor them." For the first time, Isabel understood her entire life hinged on obedience to these outside, invisible forces. Could she trust them?

Lourdes rubbed Florida Water between her palms, and she passed her hands over Isabel's body before flicking the negative energy into a glass bowl. "Go ahead," she said. "Begin with the Lord's Prayer."

Isabel recited the words from memory. The other devotees in the room joined her, lifting their chanting voices in unison. Prayers filled the small basement, rising above the smell of fresh herbs, candle wax, and grated coconut.

At the end of their prayer, Lourdes rang the altar bell to call the *Egun*. With one hand, she held a burning cigar as a smoke offering, and with the other hand, she turned pages of a prayer book and said the names of the *Moyugba*.

Lourdes taught her that the *Egun* were the intermediaries. Without the help of the ancestors, the *orisha* guardians wouldn't even talk. She said if Isabel wanted the protection of her ancestors, and if she wanted to continue working with the *orishas*, she needed to reconcile the bad blood between her and her father. "Do us all a favor, and honor him with the *bóveda*," she said. "Make peace with your past. Even spirits don't work for free." But it wasn't that simple. Isabel hadn't dealt with the bitterness and the deeply rooted mistrust she harbored against her father, against all fathers, and perhaps against all men.

Lourdes began first, saying the names of her dead ancestors. "José Luis Rodriguez Navaez, Carlos Rodriguez Navaez, Lymari Rodriguez Colón."

"Ramon Gómez Dávila, Maria Gómez Martínez," said a gray-haired man beside her. He looked prayerful as he spoke, and a deep line creased between his eyes.

"Pedro García Gómez," said a heavyset woman.

"Andrés López Fernández," said another.

"Mi papi, Rosendo Cruz," Isabel muttered, naming her father and inwardly hoping he wouldn't manifest. The memories of her father still stung, filling her with a sense of dread. His demands lingered in her head and weighed heavy on her heart years after his death. His words haunted her, but this was entirely different. Here, she was not exorcising psychological ghosts. She was inviting real ghosts to appear before her eyes.

Devotees spoke other names, names going as far back as Africa, tossing each name into the air like invisible coins. More hymns. More prayers. Smoky incense blended with the smell of cigar.

The first time her papi made contact from the other side, he spoke through the cowrie shells, which required that Ernesto interpret the reading. Ernesto said her papi had died in darkness and needed lifting rituals to move toward the light. He said her papi asked for her forgiveness. Part of Isabel felt sorry for the way things had ended between them. Part of her wanted nothing to do with him. She wanted him to take back the acid words he spoke to her before he died. She wanted to hear him say, *I love you,* but the *Egun* Rosendo said nothing of the sort.

Make Ocha, her papi told her through the *odu* pattern in the shells. *Complete the Asiento initiation and become a Santera priestess.* Had he come all this way from the land of the dead to tell her that? To ask forgiveness and then right away, demand more sacrifice? So typical of him, making demands, bullying her even from his coffin. Meddling.

"It's not enough," Lourdes said. "Sooner or later, you need to make things right between you and your papi. It's for your own good, your destiny." She said their lives were linked. His enlightenment was her own. "Don't wait until it's too late," said Lourdes. "You won't move on from your past by running."

Isabel understood her meaning. Disobedience resulted in dangerous consequences.

With a lit cigar in one hand, Lourdes turned the pages of a book called *Colección de Oraciones Escogidas* and began to sing the prayers in a low, clear voice.

As she prayed and sang, a woman named doña Alma stood to her feet. She looked dizzy and gripped the edge of the table to steady herself. With her eyes wide open, she strutted around the room, her mannerisms suddenly masculine and her voice guttural as an *Egun* mounted her. Among the devotees, possession was a great honor, an opportunity for the spirit world to speak, but Isabel cringed in terror, not wanting to hear what came next.

From the white table, doña Alma grabbed one of the lit cigars and began nibbling off the end. With one accusatory finger, she pointed at Isabel and spoke. "Promises, promises," she said. "But what do I get? Nothing!" It was her father's voice.

A sense of malaise washed over Isabel. Rosendo's voice gushed from doña Alma's mouth.

Horrified, Isabel sank deeper in her chair. "Papi, I'm sorry," she said, thoroughly scolded. She felt like a child again, powerless and accused. "Ungrateful," doña Alma scoffed. "I offer guidance and her *bóveda* goes covered with dust. No *cigarros*, no *caramelos*, no *café*." The words, full of irritation and disgust, spewed from her mouth. "It's unthinkable!"

"Tell him you love him," demanded Lourdes. "Tell him you're sorry."

Doña Alma took a bite from the cigar and swallowed. She crossed her arms in front of her chest and arched her eyebrows, waiting for Isabel to speak.

"I'll try to do better," Isabel said reluctantly.

"I wander in thick darkness," said doña Alma. "You can't imagine the hunger, yet you feed me nothing. You light no candles. You let me starve."

"Say it," said Lourdes. She told Isabel to tell him she loved him. "Do it now," she said.

"I can't." Tears slipped down Isabel's face. "I just can't."

"*Sangana*, you sabotage your own path," Lourdes snapped. "You want to be haunted by his unhappiness for the rest of your life?"

With eyes wide and full of fear, she looked from doña Alma to Lourdes. Her throat cracked, and her chest tightened. Her tongue was lead. Her lips parted, but the words wouldn't shape in her mouth.

In frustration, Lourdes asked the *Egun* to forgive Isabel. She said she needed guidance and protection, and promised Isabel would make things right.

"Ha!" doña Alma said. "Too little, too late. I offer an olive branch, and I'm ignored."

"Please, Papi. I didn't mean to offend you."

"Then get your act together."

"Yes, whatever you want," said Isabel. "I'll get what you want. Cigars."

"Rum, too," said doña Alma.

"Yes, of course."

Doña Alma spoke like a belligerent child, sweat glistening on her chest. With her fist, she slammed the table. "*Tembleque* and Coca-Cola."

The water in the glass goblets trembled.

"Yes, yes. Tembleque with cinnamon, Papi, just the way you like it. Whatever you want." Isabel clenched her jaw, but agreed to each of his demands.

"I will not be forgotten," doña Alma said.

"I won't forget," she said. That seemed to be the big problem. No matter what Ernesto and Lourdes said, Isabel found it impossible to forget. She could hardly speak to her father when he was alive. How could she pray and venerate the man now that he was dead?

"You'd better smarten up and listen," said Lourdes. "You can't keep ignoring him forever."

Isabel closed her eyes for a moment, trying to surrender the anger she felt about her papi's demands.

"Tell your papi you'll keep your covenant with him," Lourdes said through clenched teeth.

Isabel took a deep breath. "I promise," she said.

"Good girl," said doña Alma. "Maybe I'll give you a second chance. Is it too much to expect a little honor, a little respect? Tend to my *bóveda* and I'll guide you. Together, we're a force to be reckoned with."

That night, many other ancestors manifested. Some through Lourdes, some through other men and women in the room. They gave warnings, prophesied troubles, prescribed remedies for the sick, and made demands. Here, the reciprocal relationship between the living and the dead was a requisite for both blessings and protection. When it was over, the devotees hugged and wiped tears from their faces. Two women helped doña Alma clear the white table, fold the linen, and carefully shelve the glasses. On the patio, they sat in plastic chairs and balanced bowls of *sancocho* on their knees, eating the hearty soup while analyzing the more cryptic messages from their ancestors.

Lourdes smiled indulgently. "Stubborn, mija." She took another sip from her stew. "Bad blood or not, it's best to forgive."

Doña Alma, one of the better storytellers, joined them on the porch, and Lourdes asked her to tell the *Pataki* about the buffalo and the leopard.

Doña Alma took a deep breath, set her empty bowl beside her feet, and told Isabel the *Pataki*.

"Long ago, *Orisha* Oko lost his patience with the buffalo because the buffalo couldn't plow the earth. 'You're so slow, a good-for-nothing,' *Orisha* Oko said. He chided the buffalo for sinking into the mud and said his enemy, the leopard, would have no trouble plowing the land.

"Wanting to prove himself, the buffalo challenged the leopard to a duel in three days' time. The leopard roared and mocked the buffalo. He sharpened his claws and teeth and threatened to rip out his heart. During the three days, the buffalo sharpened his own horns and rolled in mud and hay. Once again, the *Orisha* Oko criticized him, calling him a dirty pig. Upon seeing him three days later, the leopard said, 'You are fatter than ever. I will have a mighty feast!' Three times, the leopard tried to sink his teeth into the buffalo, but each time, he penetrated only mud. *Orisha* Oko admitted that the buffalo was indeed a clever beast to outwit the leopard. When the time came for the buffalo to slaughter the leopard, he took pity on his enemy and horned him only one time. The leopard limped away, but he lived and learned his lesson."

"What lesson was that?" said Isabel.

Lourdes smirked. "That people aren't always what they seem. You think you're so tough, but maybe it's time you show your papi mercy like the buffalo."

"I'll try," she said halfheartedly.

Lourdes patted her shoulder with one hand. "The *Egun* are sensitive, mija. Do yourself a favor and listen. You are quick to rage, but slow to listen."

Isabel was full of doubt. If she did pacify him with the *Asiento*, would he truly help her and then leave in peace? Ultimately, it was her choice, her free will. "And what if I don't obey?"

Lourdes didn't hesitate. "Disaster," she said.

GOLPE DE SANGRE

Puerto Rico
1937

The cocks appeared to be waltzing, until the brown leghorn staggered in the pit. Paula stood ringside, assessing the bloody birds, when she saw Rosendo through a cloud of tobacco smoke. She hesitated and peered apprehensively toward the cockpit. She felt safe as long as she stayed in the roaring crowd of spectators.

Then, he was no longer visible, lost in a frenzy of cockers making bets. She searched for him among the masculine faces contorted in mania. When he appeared at her side, squinting in the smoke light, she paled at the sight of him.

"What do you think you're doing here?" he asked.

"I didn't know what else to do." Paula lifted her palm between them, and took a step away. She glanced at the other men nervously and lowered her voice. "I need to speak with you."

"I have a mind to drag you out of this arena right now," he said. He raised his eye brows, propositioning her.

"Don't come near me."

"Jesus, wipe that look off your face." He spoke through gritted teeth and swatted her away. "Go on, then. Who needs you? Get out of here." She took a step back but didn't leave. "Are you looking for trouble?"

She'd been taught that the arena, with its rowdy shouting, gambling, and drinking, was no place for a respectable woman, but it seemed ridiculous for him to be the one warning her away. For weeks, she'd been working like a mule, trying not to think of him, but he had haunted her every thought. She felt suffocated when she smelled his skin in the damp soil. When she yanked the weeds at her brother's house, clearing the ground for the *yautía*, her fingers ached with the memory of trying to pry him off her. One sleepless night, she thought she heard his voice in the hoot of a screech owl. In the embers of a glowing coal, she glimpsed the shape of his nose and lips. Now, she stood within arm's reach, squinting in the dust and smoke, and as much as she wanted to retreat, she forced herself to confront him.

"Did you hear me?" he said. "Leave."

"I won't," she shouted over the voices of the men. "I can't. I have nowhere else to go."

"Go home."

"I can't."

"What are you talking about?"

"My brother. He kicked me out."

She saw him consider this for a moment, all the fury draining from his face.

"Why would he do that?" said Rosendo.

"Don't. Don't even pretend you care."

"I do care."

"He said I dishonored his house." Panic welled in her eyes, but she composed herself. "I'm pregnant. I tried to hide it, but Luz Marí knew it straight away."

One of the gamecocks fell, and the men around them cheered.

"Like I said, you shouldn't be here." His words were slow, steady, but he grabbed her by the elbow and tried to prod her away from the arena.

She pulled out of his grip, scratching his forearm until it drew a thin trickle of blood. "Don't touch me." In her small fist, she wielded a hatpin like a dagger.

"Goddamn you." Rosendo removed his fedora and ran a hand through his matted hair, an indignant smile on his lips. "Don't you do that again." He wiped away the hairline of blood on his denim pants.

"I'm serious. I told you not to touch me," she said.

"Fine, have it your way." He turned to walk away from her.

"I need money," she said, shouting at his back.

He turned to look at her. "Who doesn't?"

He looked her up and down, taking in the full scope of her dress, damp with sweat. She felt self-conscious, aware of the yellow look in her complexion, the dark trenches under her eyes like two hollow moons. He glanced at the small, worn-out suitcase by her side.

"You've changed," he said.

He had done this, she thought. She looked blindly at the bloody birds pitted in the ring.

He said, "Have you heard news from Alberto?"

It had been over a month since he'd left for Ponce, and she'd heard nothing.

Feathers stuck to her sandals. "It doesn't matter now. I don't want him to see me. Not like this. I can't wait around here anymore." Tears slipped down her furious cheeks. She sucked in deep gulps of the foul air. "I need to leave. It's a small town."

"I wouldn't know a thing about it," he said.

"You bastard."

Rosendo sprung on her, his expression enraged. "You," he said, emphasizing each word like a nail, "don't you call me that, don't you ever."

She fought back tears. "And what about this baby? What will people call it?"

"That's your problem. Now get the hell out of my face."

Her lipstick-less mouth quivered. "But I have nowhere else to go, nothing." Luz Marí had said she should find the man who damaged her and make him take her away. But she didn't want that. She just needed the money to get out of Fajardo herself. Alone. "You said you don't lose," she said. "I need a win."

"You think you can just bet and win your ticket out of here, is that it?" He spoke to her as if she were a child. "You don't know the first thing about a winning cock."

"But you do. You told me that yourself."

"Forget it. Don't you have an aunt or a cousin? Someone from your church to take you in?"

"No, no one. Not like this . . . not disgraced."

"Shit." He spat into the dust at their feet. "Damn your family. Damn Alberto, too, for leaving in the first place. Damn your legalism and this whole backward island."

In silence, she watched a handler spit a mouthful of *aguadiente* over the head of a bird. Then the handler placed the whole chicken head in his mouth and sucked. Paula didn't understand the ritual, but tried to focus her mind on the sucking and blowing instead of the humiliation of having to go to Rosendo for help.

A referee shouted, "Get ready," and the handler released fresh roosters into the ring, taunted, agitated birds.

"If you could double, maybe triple what I've already saved," she spoke quickly, glancing at the ring.

"Even if you had the money, where would you go?" he said.

"San Juan. I can't stay here shaming my family."

"Take off alone? No, that's a mistake," he said. "A death wish."

Her body trembled as she spoke. "I'd rather die than stay here. What if Alberto does come home? What then? How do I explain? He'll kill you when he finds out what you've done."

"Or die trying," he said.

"In the end, one of you will be dead. The other will land in jail," she said. "I won't let that happen. He deserves better."

"Better than you?"

"Yes."

"So this is for him? This is your grand plan? You got it all figured out, is that it? How are you gonna raise a baby alone?"

"That's my business. Will you help me or not?"

"Make the bet yourself. I want no part in it."

"But I can't."

"Sure you can. It's not complicated."

"It's a sin."

He laughed. "You can't be serious?"

"Gambling is a sin. But you . . . You could . . ." She reached into a frayed change purse, and pulled out two weeks' worth of cleaning money, and shoved the crinkled bills forward in her fist. "Take it."

"Calm down," he said. "I need to think."

"Please, just take it."

"Christ," he said. "Fine. I'll help you."

Paula let out a deep breath as she surrendered the money. "It's every last dollar I have."

He grimaced and shoved the bills into his pocket. "Don't move." He stepped closer to the cockpit and gestured with his fingers: *100 to 20 on the speckled cock.*

The spectating men yelled and held up fingers, showing the odds. Their dusty faces contorted as they screamed and sweat dripped down their temples. Rosendo placed a bet on the speckled cock, as Paula's eyes darted from the birds to the men. She bit her lower lip and wrapped her arms around her waist to watch.

In the ring, a red bird and a speckled cock, the one Rosendo had bet on, squared off. With sharp tortoiseshell spurs taped to their legs, the brawling cocks clawed and nipped at each other. The red bird distended his neck and swiped in steely fury, but missed the chest of the speckled cock.

The spur on the speckled brown rooster dangled, a disadvantage, and the men roared in both delight and horror.

"¡*Cabrón!*" Rosendo screamed.

Paula's speckled cock slashed defensively, and the red bird staggered toward the low, circular wall.

Beside Rosendo, Paula had closed her eyes, but her lips moved in silent mutterings.

"Don't tell me you're praying?" he scoffed. "I thought you said it was a sin?"

"Shut up," she said. Glaring at the arena, she shouted, "Trap him, trap him!" pounding her fist into her thigh.

Just then, the red bird thrust into the neck of the speckled bird and blood dripped from its beak. Rosendo clenched every muscle.

Exhausted, pacing wearily around the edge, the speckled bird almost collapsed. Men leaned over the wall and beckoned the bird back into the fight. Paula and Rosendo watched in dreaded anticipation.

The red cock ran headlong, jumped into the air, and crushed his spurs through the eye and into the brain of Paula's last hope.

"!*Golpe de sangre!*" shouted Rosendo.

The dank air smelled of men and fried plantains and cigars and bitter loss. She wanted to vomit. "It's over? That's it?" Paula looked stunned. "Christ." The word was both a prayer and a curse.

She backed from the ring, her lips parted in a delirious, forgotten word. She tripped and collided with a handler. The handler hefted a canvas sack over his head, and from inside the bag, a struggling bird squawked. Paula let out a startled yelp and fell.

Rosendo helped her to her feet. "Are you all right?" He steadied her, resting his hand on her lower back.

"Don't." She shoved him. Feathers slick with blood scattered across the packed dirt floor, and she almost slipped a second time. He reached his hands out to caution her, but she slapped them away. "You lost on purpose. You did it on purpose." Tears smeared dusty streaks down her cheeks.

He looked as if he didn't know what to say, and she had an impulse to smack him. She clenched her fists, kept them pressed to her sides. He had bet on the weaker bird. She had relinquished every red cent.

"Believe whatever the hell you want, but you're wrong," he said. "I was trying to help."

"You told me yourself. A sure thing. Isn't that what you said?"

"Maybe I did, but it doesn't work that way. Men say lots of things sometimes, especially when they're trying to impress a beautiful woman. I told you to find another way. I tried to warn you."

"Oh, God," she moaned. "I need to get out of here. I need air."

"Come." He extended his hand. "Let's go."

She looked confused. "Go? You mean with you?"

"Yes, let's go home. You look ill." His eyes were steady, his tone authoritative.

She laughed hysterically and wiped her eyes with the back of her hand. "You're out of your mind."

"Am I?" He pressed in on her, uncomfortable, hulking. She could smell the reek of his body. "The way I see it, we're family now. That baby inside you is a Cruz. It's mine."

She shuddered.

"Look, I'll help you," he said in the gentle tone she distrusted. "You can stay with me at my mother's. Just for a few days until we can figure out a way to win the money back."

"Stay with you?"

"With my mother. You're family now. She'll help."

"And you?" She stared at him.

"I didn't mean to lose the money," he said. "I swear. I feel awful about it. About a lot of things. Believe me, I won't let a child of mine starve. I said I would help, and I will. You have my word."

"That means nothing to me. I don't trust a single word that comes out of your mouth."

"One chance." He clenched his jaw. "I never knew my father, and the last thing I want on this earth is for any child of mine to walk a single day in my shoes. I could live with just about anything, but not that. Not a bastard. Give me one chance." The sincerity with which he spoke surprised her. "I'll make it right."

Like the *amarradores*, the men who bind the blade to the rooster's leg, he reached for her slowly, tentatively, and wound his fingers around her arm. With his other hand, he lifted her suitcase and led her trembling out of the arena. They walked together into the ghost light of the village streets.

*

"You have to marry the girl," doña Carmen said. In a more sympathetic tone, she said to Paula, "Your brother came to the house this afternoon in an uproar."

Paula felt sick to her stomach. "Oh, God, what did he say?"

"He's insisting Rosendo take responsibility."

Rosendo smirked and sucked his teeth.

Carmen sat hunched over a washboard and scrubbed. "She's no *puta*. She's a good girl from a decent family. She's your problem now."

"Calm down," he said. "I take care of my own."

"And you better clear out. You can't stay under this roof. God help me, when your brother comes home—"

"*If* he comes home," Rosendo said.

"He's alive, and he's coming back."

"You talking about Alberto or Jesus? I get confused sometimes, the way you worship that boy."

Carmen scoffed. "A mother knows these things. And when he does come home, he'll cut you to ribbons. It'd serve you right."

Rosendo burst out laughing. "Let him try."

She coughed and spat at the dirt beside his boots. "You're as bad as they come." Her lips pressed into a tight, hard line.

"Don't blame me," he said. "I'm not like Paula here. I don't come from a *decent* family." He looked hard into her eyes.

"Go to hell," she said, but there was no longer anger in her words, only a deep sadness.

"I'll clear out," he said. "There's no life during the dead time anyway. Got five more months at the mill, but maybe it's not even worth it. The pay's shit."

"Please go," she said. "Before you bring more trouble into this house."

He nodded, shoved his hands into his pockets, and looked off into the distance where the mountains loomed higher than the clouds.

"Straighten yourself up, son." Doña Carmen's watery eyes looked deep into Rosendo's face. "You want to be a peasant your whole life?"

"No." His voice sounded childish in its defiance.

"I have thirty-five dollars saved," she said. "Take Paula, and make a better man of yourself."

"I don't want your money." He kicked the dirt, sneering at her.

"It's not for you." Flies swarmed around a metal barrel filled with water. She tilted the barrel with both hands, spilling murky soap water around her sandaled feet. "Take it," she said. "It's for my grandchild. You can both stay here the one night. After that, I want you cleared out."

That night Paula slept in the hammock Alberto had left behind. Carmen's shack felt sticky with heat, and the burlap scratched against her skin. She couldn't remember the last time she'd slept soundly. A rusted pot caked in urine lay on the floor beside her, but even with a full bladder, she didn't consider it. She needed fresh air. Privacy. She slipped out of the hammock, and the floor creaked beneath her bare feet. For a moment, she stood motionless, letting her eyes and ears adjust to the darkness. In the two other hammocks, Carmen and Rosendo were dark, pod-shaped figures suspended over the floor. Cocoons of heavy breathing, farts, and scratching. Paula heard the quick-footed patter of an iguana on the tin roof.

Outside, a billion specks of light illuminated the night sky. She imagined the stars falling one by one to the earth, sullen, hissing as they sank. The thought reminded her of Alberto. Before he had left for Ponce, a foreboding feeling had shadowed her for weeks. She longed to speak with him, to know he was all right. She stood for a moment on the porch, watching the sky, but nothing happened. There were no shooting stars, no signs to show the way. She arched her back and sucked in a deep breath of night air. A breeze blew in from the sea, and she felt the gooseflesh rise on her skin.

The wood creaked, and Rosendo stepped outside. He didn't acknowledge her. He simply unzipped his trousers and urinated off the edge of the porch. He kept his eyes on the stars. "Wish I'd paid more attention to their names when I was a kid," he said, zipping up. "Elba knew all the stars' names and patterns. She tried to teach me, but I could never sit still."

He sat on the porch and hunched over a packet of tobacco. He opened a sheet of cigarette paper and began sprinkling stringy tobacco along the crease. "Block the wind," he said.

She didn't want to be close to him, but she obeyed. She sat on the porch, her back toward Rosendo as he rolled the paper. When he was finished, he struck a match and lit the end of his cigarette. Paula turned as the brief light illuminated his high cheekbones and the deep circles under his eyes. He must have sensed her nervousness because he moved away from her and leaned against the hut.

"I thought I'd fix up this roof," he said. "Maybe start a cash crop. A man could squat here forever. Too bad."

From the mountains, it all looked closer, as if the night sky were lowering to meet her. Or was she rising up? Her body felt weightless, free of skin, bone, and blood. "It looks so close," she said.

"The veil between this world and the others is paper thin."

"What?"

"Nothing," he said. "Just something Elba used to say."

His words reminded her of the veil dividing the Holy of Holies from the rest of the Temple in Jerusalem. Ever since she was a girl, she had been taught that her body was the new temple. If she pulled back the inner curtain of herself, were there worlds within? Would she stand face to face with the divine? "The body is the temple of God," she said.

"If Elba wanted, she could simply slip out of her body, wander up and down the mountain paths under the stars while the whole world slept all around."

Paula imagined ghostly feet meandering dirt lanes. She imagined snapping the strand of hair that grounded her own body. She would become an untethered kite, her disembodied shadow-self blowing down the mountainside. But what would be the point? She'd already seen everything in this village. Sleeping peasants, empty footpaths, overgrown bushes and trees.

She thought of Alberto. So far away. If she could, she would find him. She would peek into every house in the city if she had to. Find him and touch him like a dream.

"Have you ever done it?" she said. "Left your skin?"

"Too risky," said Rosendo, "leaving your body far behind. An empty open vessel attracts trouble."

The thought unsettled her. "What kind of trouble?"

"I knew a man," he said, "an old fool, who returned to his body only to find it occupied by someone else making love to his wife." He grinned. "Think of the possibilities."

"You'd have to be crazy to leave your skin and go traipsing through these woods," she said.

"Or desperate."

She thought he looked like the most desperate man she'd ever seen. She understood that for a man, catching a girl on the cusp of womanhood held the pleasure of a succulent *lechón*. Is that all he saw in her? Split-roasted meat? Her own ancestors, the Taíno, had invented the method of roasting meat over smoky pits. From his eyes and light skin, she could see the Spaniard in him. The Spaniards had dominated the Taíno like chattel to be owned. Spaniards used the Taíno women as vessels to be occupied. Inside him raged the abuses of a thousand ancestors. He had used her, and she felt gutted, empty like the pig.

*

In the morning, Rosendo packed his small canvas sack, and Paula sat beside Carmen to speak privately. "I don't want this," she said in a whisper.

Carmen squeezed the girl's hand. "*Ay, bendita*, what choice do you have?"

She knew doña Carmen was right. She had no choice. She would go with Rosendo to San Juan, and then she would run. If she could hold out long enough to earn a little money, she could make a plan and escape. For now, she submitted. For now, she bit her tongue.

Paula and Rosendo used his mother's money and took a *público* taxi to San Juan. He had ignored her despondence in the taxi and had spoken lightheartedly of the future. The farther they drove away from Fajardo, the more encouraged he seemed. He said as soon as they arrived in the city, he would pay the woman at the tavern to make Paula a chicken broth, and said he would buy her a new nylon dress and a bottle of perfume.

"Save your money," she said coolly. "I'm not your sweetheart, and I have no interest in pretending." It gave her pleasure to watch his face fall. -

For five dollars, they rented a room at a dingy hotel above a tavern. "Our honeymoon," he said. "It's not the Condado Beach Hotel, but it's not all bad."

Paula had grown silent during the drive. Now she felt disembodied, far, far away.

"Things are tight now," he said, "but I have a watch I can hock." He frowned when she didn't answer. "Won't you say something?"

"Get a bottle of Flit," she said quietly.

"What for?"

"Because after one night in this place, we'll need to pour it over our heads to get rid of the lice."

"Don't worry," he said. "We'll manage. I'll find factory work in the city, and we'll find a better place."

"Here's the thing," she said, placing one hand on her hip. "I didn't come here to set up house with you. You might be the father of this baby, but you are certainly not my husband and this is not our honeymoon."

"To hell with you," he said. "I've tried to be nice, but no matter what I do, you look fit to kill."

"What did you expect? That you would bring me here, and I would forget everything you've done?"

"I need a drink," he said. "Let's go down to the bar."

"I told you." She sounded exasperated. "I don't drink."

"And I don't care," he said. "You can watch."

In the tavern, they sat at the bar. He ordered two Cuba Libres and proceeded to drink both himself. Women with elaborately curled hair, scandalously low-cut dresses, and powdered faces danced the mambo with American sailors straight off the navy ships. Rosendo watched the dancers, absorbed.

"Do you dance?" he asked her, halfheartedly.

"Adventists don't dance," she said. She resented being dragged into a bar, and it angered her to see him gawking over these other women in front of her face.

"Ave Maria, girl! You need to lighten up. God forbid you add a little spice to your life."

She rolled her eyes and watched the dancers, fluid and pulsing, and couldn't help admire their beauty.

"Mambo means conversation with the gods," he said. "You feel it right? Admit it, *negrita*, I know you got some Africa in those bones."

Her stomach growled. Embarrassed, she wrapped her arms around her chest. "I'm hungry," she said. She resented being dependent on him, on any man, and she needed to figure out a way to earn money for herself.

He reached into his pocket, pulled out a dime, and held it between two fingers. "Be sweet." She grabbed the dime and stepped off the bar stool, but before she could walk away, he grabbed her wrist. "I'll be right here," he said. "If you're not back in fifteen minutes, I'm dragging you back by your hair."

From a pushcart vendor on the street, she bought two cents' worth of bread, milk, and a bar of chocolate. She ate the bread first, then crossed the cobblestone street, breaking off small squares of chocolate with her fingers and savoring the rich flavor on her tongue. She needed to calm down, to gather her strength before facing him again. Surely, she had ten minutes to walk, to think.

At first, she walked aimlessly, admiring the grillwork of iron gates and the balconies with cascading flowers. She knew no one in *Viejo* San Juan, and she had never seen so many people. Still, she felt lonelier than ever.

An automobile honked behind her, and along with a young girl selling mangoes, she pressed her back along a cement building to allow the driver to pass on the narrow road. Inside the car, she noticed tourists with large-brimmed hats and white gloves. Perhaps she could get a job as a maid in a hotel? Maybe she could work on a steamer ship and sail away? She did not pay attention to the street signs or whether she turned left or right. She walked down alleys, picking up her pace, daring herself to disappear. *Go farther, and you'll starve. Go farther, and you'll be all alone in the world.* Fifteen minutes, he'd said.

Now she was at the tip of Viejo San Juan in the Cemetery of St. Mary Magdalene of Pazziz, high above the rocky coastline. The cemetery banked along the Atlantic, nestled between the twin fortresses of El Morro and San Cristobal, its white tombs contrasting against the brilliant blues of the sky and sea. Several feet below, breakers rushed toward the coast and smashed against stone. She could smell the salt in the breeze, hear the deep bestial blast of a steamer ship.

She gulped down the milk, thirstier than she'd realized. She imagined throwing the glass over the bluffs, watching it shatter against the rocks. She imagined a splendid leap, her own body breaking. She turned her palm up in surrender and prayed, *Father, if you are willing, take this cup from me.* That's when she noticed Rosendo under the white arches, leaning against the cemetery gates. He watched her, his posture casual and relaxed, as if he had all the time in the world. He tipped his hat, eyes bright and mocking. Had he followed her? Had he been there the whole time?

It made no sense to hide, but she instinctively cowered behind a gravestone, panic choking out thought.

Rosendo unfastened his calf-leather belt, a secondhand import from Italy, and clenched it in his fist. She crawled on hands and knees over a grave marker—crude etchings scrawled into stone. Other markers stood waist high. Whitewashed crosses, rows of mausoleums, tombs, and statues of the saints.

Rosendo stood at the gate only a few feet away, scowling. Why didn't he enter and come after her? The gate wasn't locked. Were his superstitions so powerful they prevented him? She sucked in deep breaths of air, and caught the scent of fresh flowers strewn on a grave.

"I can wait here all day," Rosendo shouted. "All night if I have to."

Paula's eyes darted around the cemetery, looking for another way out. She considered his threat. If he wouldn't follow her into the cemetery, would he really guard the gates? Even after dark?

"Paula, I'm sorry. Dammit." He smashed the gate with his fist, eyes scanning wildly over the graves. "I'm doing my best to make right by you, but Christ, you're not making any of this easy."

"Go away."

"It's our wedding night for God's sake!"

"Stop saying that. Leave me alone," she screamed. "I don't want you. I've changed my mind. I don't want your help."

"Think of our baby. My baby."

She said nothing.

"Come on," he said. "We can't stay here."

"Please, for the love of God, just go." She wanted him to leave, but then what? Then she would be alone with nowhere to turn for help. Pregnant, disgraced, destitute. Doña Carmen's words echoed in her ears. What choice do you have? Every choice had been stripped from her.

"Go away," she screamed.

"And leave you here? At night the *paleros* raid the cemeteries for their dark magic."

"I don't care."

"They open tombs and dig up bones for their religious rituals."

"You're lying. Everything you say is a lie."

"I've seen it with my own eyes when I was a boy. The concrete slabs ransacked. Skulls stolen."

She scanned the many tombs topped with elaborate sculptures. She didn't want to believe him.

"You think I'd just leave you?" he said. "What kind of man leaves his wife and baby alone?"

Paula wondered if she could hold out until dark. Maybe under the cover of night, with God's grace, she could sneak away. The sun beat down from overhead, clear and bright. It would be hours before sunset, she thought. If she returned with Rosendo now, she knew there would be no escaping his lunacy, maybe not ever. She scanned the overgrown bushes and weeds looking for another way out. Beyond the cemetery, she saw the silhouette of the barrio outside the historic walls. If she banged on a door, would someone help? Or would they take advantage of a desperate country girl, alone in the city?

Rosendo shouted. "They'll be coming, you know. After dark. This land is marked for death." He pleaded with her now. "Look, I won't hurt you." He said the words softly through clenched teeth. From a distance, several tourists watched them as if they were part of the historic landmark. She could see him breathing heavily, wiping the sweat from his face. "I promise. I'm not mad." He sounded more sober, begging like a child. "I just want you to come back. Stop all this foolishness. Be reasonable. *Mi amor*, I'm sorry."

In the end, she relented, and as they walked back to the hotel, Rosendo walked close beside her, his eyes blazing. She heard him mutter something under his breath, a cruel sound, but she didn't turn to look at his face. Later, that night, people in the neighboring rooms could hear the whip of the belt, the crack and smack against skin. Some poked their heads out of doors and said things like, *Sometimes a woman asks for it and needs to be punished*, or *Man and wife have the right to kill each other if they want. It's none of our business.*

In the morning, Rosendo promised to be a better man. He caressed her cheek and kissed the fiery welts across the back of her thighs. In the months that followed, her stomach grew melon-shaped, and she ran away and hid a second and a third time, always in the cemetery, the one place he wouldn't enter. Each time, she relented as the sun set, only to find herself dragged back in the end and beaten without mercy. By the time their daughter Juanita was born, she had stopped running altogether. Her time had run out.

At first, Rosendo basked in fatherhood. He got a job in a factory like he said, rented a one-room stilt house and provided a layette for the baby. At high tide, the ocean reached far under their decrepit house, and Paula feared she and the baby would be carried out to sea. When he felt calm, his gentle words provided no comfort to her. She'd heard them a thousand times before. She felt lost in the wilderness of his mood swings, from laughter to fury, triggered by the smallest things. A stale piece of bread, an admiring stare directed at her from a man in town. He could be gentle and kind one moment, laughing or whistling a folk song. Then, something unseen triggered his rage, something she couldn't predict, but sensed in her bones, restless like birds before the eruption of a mountain.

She had been through enough cycles with Rosendo to know his rage. She knew he could momentarily rein in his temper, days at a time, but she also knew no amount of his gentle coaxing or apologies could be trusted. When his anger lashed out, it possessed him with a sadistic force.

After the baby came the Second World War, the marches against the draft, and the telegraph that doña Carmen had died of typhoid. There was no funeral, but Rosendo paid three dollars a month to rent her cemetery plot. "It's the least I can do," he said. "She gave us every penny she had." Years later, when he could no longer afford to pay for the plot, grave diggers dug up the dust and bones, placed what remained in a small plastic bag, and dropped the bag into an unmarked hole.

A midwife had helped deliver Juanita in the house on stilts. The baby resembled Paula with wavy black hair and dark eyes, but when Paula was pregnant a second time, Rosendo accused her of running around with other men while he worked in the factory. "Don't think you'll get away with putting the horns on me," he said, shoving two quinine tablets into her mouth. He forced her to drink water, tears streaming down her face, and Paula gagged on the tablets and swallowed. When he left for the tavern, she put her finger into her throat and forced herself to vomit up the pills. When their son Angelito was born, Rosendo refused to give the boy his last name.

As a small girl, Juanita was Paula's helper, a little mother tending to the cooking, the cleaning, and the siblings who followed. After Angelito, Celia was born, a fiery girl with a waterfall laugh and a knuckle punch. Next came Rosa and Joseph. Then when she thought she was too old for children, a woman from her church laid hands on Paula's belly and prophesied twins, Jacob and Esau. Isabel came last.

With each new year, there seemed to be a new baby. A ceaseless line of infants nursing at her breast, a toddler on her hip, a child at her heel. After a decade, her body morphed into wide, soft curves she no longer recognized. Even the smell of her own body struck her as foreign. She smelled of breast milk, chicken stock, and the Lifebuoy soap she used on her skin as well as on the laundry.

Each new child anchored her to Rosendo. The gravitational pull of her motherly devotion kept her orbiting around her children as if she were the dying star in their ever-expanding universe.

Paula remembered her own great-grandmother. She remembered the stories of how dogs chased her down in a field when she was only nine years old. Her great-grandmother said she ran in terror but was overcome by their barking and snapping at her legs. She said the Spaniards used ropes to tie her wrists and ankles. Said she was bound and branded and showed Paula the scars to prove it.

From her great-grandmother, she'd learned there was no stopping the things God had no intention of stopping. So Paula didn't fight against what she saw as her fate. Instead, she learned to read Rosendo's moods, their intensity and ferocity. She became an expert in the things that pleased and displeased him. Learned the times it was safe to be noticed, and when it was best to be invisible, out of the way. Like the slave master's dogs, her love for her children kept her from running away from him for good.

THE WATCHERS

City Island, NY
1983

Day and night, they nested in the trees. From her bedroom window, Esther saw the slender figures balancing like trapeze artists, dangling along the telephone wires. Milky skin, eyes like puddles of oil, silent. She called them the Watchers, and they filled the hollow spaces between branches. They perched like gargoyles over the doorframes and scurried along the fence post on all fours.

"They aren't real," she told herself under her breath, but gooseflesh pricked her arms. Her skin and blood believed. Go away, she wanted to say to the air, but didn't dare speak the words aloud. It was dangerous to offend the spirits. What if they heard? What if they spoke back?

When she asked her mother about the Watchers, she secretly hoped that her mother would dismiss them as figments of her imagination. Instead, her mother told her stories about the *orishas* as if she spoke of members of their own family. She explained that the *orishas* were one with the elements. She told stories of ancestor guides and guardian angels. She reminded Esther that Changó was the god of lightning, and his wife, Oshún, was the force of water. She said they were among the ancient race, the fallen ones from heaven who went by many names: Watchers, *orishas*, principalities of the air, the keepers, the guardians, the guides. Esther learned they were the guards of the doors, the portals between the worlds and the heavenly realms.

123

She wanted nothing to do with the gaunt creatures lurking in the periphery of her day to day, but despite her best attempts to ignore them, she heard their phantom voices calling her name through the walls. *Esther*, the voice called in the voice of her mother. *Esther*, a breathy voice, male this time. *Esther*, like a knock at the door. She didn't answer. At home after dark, she turned on every light in the house, walking from room to room with her nerves on edge. She closed the blinds, drew the curtains, and avoided her own reflection in the windows. Still, she couldn't escape the sensation of their presence.

In Alfred Hitchcock's film *The Birds*, crows massed on a jungle gym outside a schoolhouse. They swooped down from the sky and alighted on the metal bars, waiting for the bell to dismiss the children. Esther's fear of the Watchers took shape and shadowed her like dark birds. Over her shoulder, behind the door, under the bed, in the dark. She couldn't outrun the crows of her own making. No matter how hard she squeezed her eyes shut, they pecked through her thin skin. Relentless, illusory devils. Milky-white and all eyes.

Her mother told her that the *orishas* crossed the Caribbean Sea on slave ships from the Yoruba kingdom in Africa. "Changó came to Puerto Rico mounted on the tongues of slaves," she said. She described how the kidnapped Yoruba people muttered his name in prayer as their prostrate bodies pitched and fell on violent waves. Esther imagined the foamy surf buck and the Yoruba people screaming out to their ancestors and saints.

Her mother handed her a cup of milk and a stack of Oreo cookies in a paper towel, and Esther sat on a kitchen barstool swirling a cookie in a ceramic cup. "Are Oreos named after *orishas*?" She was trying to be clever, lighten the mood, but her mother looked grim and irritated.

"*Ori* means consciousness," she said. "And *Sha* means protector."

"Like a bodyguard for your brain?"

"Like a guardian angel," her mother said. "Legions of spirits were smuggled on slave ships."

"How many is a legion?" Esther didn't like chocolate bits floating in her milk and strategically bobbed the cookie for three *Mississippis.*

"Too many to count," her mother said.

In Esther's backyard, the Long Island Sound rushed the seawall and slapped into the dock. She heard the creaking sound of heavy timber and bit into the soft cookie before prying the remaining halves apart. She scraped the creamy middle with her bottom teeth and felt the granules of sugar spread across her tongue. She said, "How do secret names travel on tongues?"

"You know, like prayer." Her mother opened the lips of the milk carton and filled her cup. "Drink your milk."

On the back of the carton, the word MISSING read in bold print. Esther glanced at the image of a black-and-white pixelated girl and the computer composite of the girl's face as a teenager. She thought of strangers in white vans and El Cuco. She thought of legions of Yoruba, women and children snatched from their beds. Missing. Even with a host of angelic protectors, her mother inhabited a world of predators, visible and invisible. Her mother's lens shaped her own, and no matter how hard Esther tried to run from her fear, a flock of clawing birds trailed at her back.

Her grandmother Paula lived to be ninety-nine years old, and as far back as she could remember, Esther observed her grandmother kneeling beside her bed each night, whispering prayers in Spanish. As a girl, she didn't understand her grandmother's words, but deep down, she knew some of those prayers were for her, and that gave her comfort. Sometimes, she knelt beside her grandmother, lowered her forehead onto her mattress, and closed her eyes. She didn't know Spanish, so she moved her lips silently, pretending. She wondered about the right words to say.

Her mother explained that prayer wasn't limited by words. "That's why some slap the sacred drum and dance," she said. "It's a prayer language, a language from the time before time. You don't always need words."

"Then how will I learn it?" Esther asked.

"You listen for it. It's all around you," her mother said. "Prayer is just one door. But there are lots of other doors. Some good, some evil."

Esther wondered about the prayer words and the other things the Yoruba smuggled aboard slave ships—secret, hidden things on tongues and in the folds of fabric. To this day, as a grown woman, she compulsively locks her front and back doors. Even as a wife and mother, her dreams are full of open doors, and in terror, she locks and relocks bolts that refused to stay shut.

Looking back, Esther didn't blame her mother for the stories that took root in the darkest creases of her imagination. Nevertheless, fear is a presence, a phantom. It takes possession, and no matter how hard you resist, it isn't removed by force.

SIGNS AND WONDERS

New York
1974

What began as an ulcer in Rosendo's big toe eventually led to his death. First, the skin on the toe cracked and pulled away. Then the foot swelled, red and warm. By the time he noticed the wound, infection had already set in. "It's just a bruise," he insisted, but doctors diagnosed him with gangrene. They said he'd lose the whole foot.

Before his surgery, the women at his storefront Pentecostal church cooked meals for the family and held an all-night prayer vigil for their beloved pastor. Members of the congregation wore coarse burlap sacks over their Sunday best, and that night there was a great filling of the Holy Spirit. The dancing in the aisles and speaking in tongues lasted for many hours. Several devotees shouted, "¡*Gracias, Señor!*" and collapsed, knocked right off their feet. More than a few shook and spasmed so hard that they wore out the carpet beneath their burlap backs.

In the morning, Paula filled a ceramic bowl with rice and beans and covered it with aluminum foil. She told her children that their papi would want them at his bedside when he woke from surgery. She slid the rice bowl into a large purse and directed her eyes at Isabel, raising her eyebrows as if to say, *Aren't you coming?*

"No way," Isabel said. "Go without me." She had nothing to say to her father. Gangrene or not, she and Rosendo were no longer on speaking terms.

127

Her mother Paula insisted that he'd want her there.

"You're wrong," said Isabel. "Having me there will only upset him." She didn't want to disobey her mother, but she wasn't ready to face her father, not yet. She imagined the hospital gown sagging around his thin, hollow chest, and the stump where a foot should be under scratchy sheets. She imagined her mother feeding her father like a child, the smell of *sofrito*, onion, and bleach filling the room. She didn't want to feel sorry for him, not even now. It didn't change things between them. It didn't take back the words he said or the years of beatings. Isabel wasn't buying the Sunday suits he now wore or the rehearsed sermons he memorized. She'd been to Broadway shows. She recognized a good performance when she saw one.

His story of a near-death experience five years earlier was simply that. A fiction. A hallucination at best. She didn't trust sudden conversions. According to his story, Tío Alberto killed him first, years before the ulcer. Only, he didn't stay killed. Instead, he woke up from the hospital bed with a fractured spine, his body in a cast, and his arm in a sling. At the time, Isabel was nineteen, and she had wished her father dead more times than she could count. Having him rise from the dead was entirely unexpected and unwelcomed.

In the furniture factory where Rosendo and Alberto worked in New York, they called the machine the spindle monster. It could rip a man's thumb off in a split second. With two steel knives spinning at ten thousand revolutions per second, the spindle monster could have a man up to his elbow before a scream escaped his lips. No one witnessed how it began, but by the end of a twelve-hour shift, the reunited brothers were fighting. In the end, Alberto shoved the spindle monster off a ledge. The older brother was crushed. Then the place went up in smoke. Some said it was from the sawdust igniting, but others said Alberto had started the fire himself.

Rosendo blacked out, and when he woke up in the hospital room, he was a changed man. Like Lazarus, he said he had risen from the dead. For what felt like hours, he had suspended between two worlds, hovering over his own body like a bat. He saw the bright tunnel of light, heard the voice of his mother Carmen, felt the love of Jesus. Isabel wasn't buying any of it.

He planted a small church in a storefront, and because he couldn't read, Paula read scripture to him, which he committed to memory. When he spoke from the pulpit, he delivered his sermons with zeal and tears, his voice hoarse with conviction.

*

Five years after the fire, on the morning of his foot surgery, Paula, Isabel's siblings, nieces, and nephews, along with several well-intentioned ladies from the Pentecostal church, sat in the hospital waiting room. Everyone but Isabel. Despite her mother's nagging and her siblings calling her a *pendeja*, she refused to see him.

She replayed the old arguments in her mind. Like the liner notes of a favorite record album, over and over again, she sifted through the details. Savored the anger. In her heart, she accused him for the hundredth time.

"People change," her mother told her. "What you choose to remember and forget, that's your business, but you're only hurting yourself."

Isabel remembered his cruelty from her childhood. It wasn't a choice. How could she forget? Especially not after he had berated her for getting knocked up and blamed her for driving Jude away. When she moved back home to her parents' apartment on Pitt Street, pregnant and dejected, he ignored her. Now as he lay dying, she felt furious at how unfair it all was. She wanted to hear him say he was sorry. She wanted him to look into her eyes and see the little girl, desperate for her father's affection. Worthy of his attention.

She had never felt more alone, more lost. She'd sabotaged her relationship with Jude the moment she set fire to the *Lady Viking*. Now, he refused to answer her calls. It dawned on her that the two most significant men in her life wanted nothing to do with her. With one phone call, Jude could send her to prison for arson.

Would she lose him, the baby, and even land in jail in one stroke? Her rage had ransacked every possible hope. She feared he despised her. If she lost the baby like the others, he'd never take her back.

*

The morning after she had set fire to the *Lady Viking*, Isabel counted the money left in her purse and prayed it was enough for a miracle. Could you compel forgiveness, force devotion, conjure love?

Isabel accompanied Lourdes to the Catholic church on Fordham Road and lit candles in front of the Blessed Virgin Mary. She stared into the statue's faded glass eyes and noticed the chipped, graceful hands in prayer. She looked over her shoulder, uneasy, but the other patrons in the pews seemed engaged in private prayers and hardly noticed her.

Lourdes kneeled in front of the altar and told Isabel to pray, so Isabel kneeled beside her. They clasped their hands and bowed their heads.

From the corner of her eye, Isabel peeked at Lourdes. "I don't know what to say. Do I pray to Mary?"

"Of course not, dear." Lourdes reminded her that when they prayed to Mary, they were really praying to Yemayá. The Catholic statue only represented their goddess, embodied her. This was how Santeros had maintained their secrecy for so many centuries.

"But what do I say, exactly?"

Lourdes sighed and told her to set an intention and say what was on her heart. "Just start already," she said. "My knees are killing me."

Isabel closed her eyes and prayed. *Please, my life is spinning out of control. Make Jude take me back. Please make him love me again.*

"Good," Lourdes said. "Now, leave the necklace."

Isabel removed a blue and crystal beaded necklace from her purse and placed it on the altar.

They made a plan to go to Orchard Beach the following day. There, they would leave a fruit offering and say the Hail Marys. Lourdes told Isabel not to worry. "Jude still cares about you,

130

otherwise he would have gone straight to the police," she said. Lourdes assured her that the goddess would protect her baby and clean up the mess she'd made with Jude.

Isabel felt relieved to hear that the Orchard Beach offering was only fruit. "That's good," she said, "because I'm running out of money. With all these gifts for the saints, I'm going broke."

"Hush," said Lourdes. "We won't get sloppy now. Money is energy, and there must be an exchange. When you work with me, we don't cut corners. That's asking for trouble." She said the sacrificial gifts were like gasoline. They were the energy that fueled the magic. "You'll see," she said. "Now, there is one more thing." She rose to her feet and pressed her palms to her lower back, arching as she spoke. "You need to make peace with your father. Your lack of forgiveness and anger corrupts your path."

In the days after the operation on his foot, Isabel wrestled with Lourdes's command. It felt easier to hate her father than to endure another moment of his rejection. Walls came easier than vulnerability, but a childlike part of her did desperately want her father's approval. Before she could make up her own mind, her sisters called to say that her papi had suffered from a fatal heart attack.

Isabel called Jude at work. "Please, don't hang up. My father's dead."

"What are you talking about?"

"This morning," she said. "He died at the hospital from a heart attack."

"Christ. I'm sorry, Isabel. How's Paula holding up?"

"She's strong, you know. She's been taking care of him for a really long time. She won't admit it, but I think she's exhausted and maybe quietly relieved. She wanted me to call you. It would mean a lot to her if you came to the funeral."

"I don't know," Jude said. They hadn't seen one another face-to-face in over a month.

"Look, I'm sorry. How many times do I have to say it?" She hoped he'd hear the sincerity in her voice. "I'm so very sorry."

"I know you are."

"It was an accident," she said. "Things between you and me got out of hand, that's all."

"I'm at work now," he said. "I gotta go."

She didn't want him to hang up. "I don't know what I was thinking. I thought . . . I just went crazy."

"This isn't a good time."

"You believe me, don't you? It was an accident."

"Right." There was a long pause before he spoke again. "You still staying at your mother's?"

"God, yes. I'm so sick of this miserable apartment," she said. "You should see me. The baby's growing."

"That's good," he said. "That's real good." His voice trailed off. "I'm glad you're okay."

"I've missed you, Jude."

He didn't answer.

"Did you hear me?"

"Look, I haven't wrapped my head around all this yet. I need time."

"Of course," she said. Isabel cradled the phone with her shoulder and rubbed one hand over her stomach. "I'll make it up to you," she said. "I don't know how, but I'll find a way. I just want our life back."

"Look, I'm sorry to hear about your father, I really am, but . . ."

Isabel started to cry. "Just come to the funeral, Jude. I'm begging you. At least say goodbye."

Jude walked into the Iglesia de Dios Pentecostal Church to pay his last respects to Rosendo. He wore a Salvation Army suit. It was too short at the ankles, but Isabel breathed a sigh of relief the moment she saw him slip into the dimly lit church. Parishioners packed the pews, so Jude grabbed a metal folding chair in the last row. She craned her neck and tried to catch his attention.

Celia could hardly finish singing her father's favorite devotion, "Yo Te Amo, Señor," before breaking down into loud sobs. Their brothers Jacob and Esau had to help her walk off the red velvet stage on account of her weeping. Isabel felt anxious to speak to Jude, and all through the service she repeatedly glanced back in his direction to make sure he hadn't left.

Her father's grown children and grandchildren gathered around the open casket, and placed arms around their mother, who looked withered and gray. Isabel stood awkwardly at a distance, not looking at her father's rigid body, not shedding a single tear. She fidgeted with her hands and hoped to God that Jude wouldn't leave before she had a chance to speak with him.

She finally got her chance after the service, in an impossibly narrow stairwell. Through a grimy window, a neon cross with the words *JESUS SAVES* emblazoned on it, flickered on and off, casting a red glow on their faces as they spoke. Isabel reached for Jude's arm, and he kissed the top of her head.

"I know I messed up," she said. "I don't want to lose you."

"Maybe you need help," he said.

Her face brightened. "I'm getting help," she said. "I'm seeing someone."

"A therapist?"

"Sort of, yes." She didn't know how to explain Lourdes. "You'd like her." She touched her hand to his face. "Look at me. You know me. It was an accident. Admit it, Jude. You need me."

"I need you like I need a hole in my head." Then he wrapped his arms around her back as she leaned her head into his chest.

"I didn't mean it," she said. "I didn't mean to do any of it."

And so, Jude forgave Isabel for setting fire to his boat. It took only two sacrificial chickens, two pigeons, a possum, a baptism, a fruit offering, and three hundred and forty-two dollars. *A bargain*, thought Isabel.

Isabel dialed her madrina to tell her the good news.

"The *orishas* are taking care of everything. Didn't I tell you not to worry?" said Lourdes.

*

I sabel spent almost every weekend with her godmother learning the rituals of Santeria. Carefully, she observed and imitated her, taking notes in her *libreta*, a small notebook she carried in her purse at all times. In her notebook, she recorded the sixty-four seashell patterns needed to read the cowrie shells, the meaning of the four coconut rinds used in divination, and the five patterns of the rinds. She noted the special herbs associated with each *orisha*, both their Spanish and English names. She made a list of sweet herbs and bitter herbs. She wrote the ingredients of the holy water baths used to destroy evil and the potions used to keep life running smoothly. Each *orisha* favored certain colors, flowers, fragrances, and animals, and she studied hard to commit these to memory. She put her faith in the magical properties of oils and spells.

Now, at six months into her pregnancy, Isabel stood in drizzling rain on Rochelle Street, City Island admiring her dream house. She stood outside the fence, shivering in the cold, and knew it was destined to be her home. "Honey, you have to get me this house," she said to Jude. She tugged playfully at his arm. "That's it. That's the one I want."

"But it's huge," he said.

She was elated. "I love it."

"It's waterfront."

"Exactly."

"It'll be a fortune."

"Trust me." Her cocky tone surprised even her. "You make an offer, and I'll get us that house." She felt giddy, knowing that with the help of her *orishas*, the possibilities were endless. The sense of power animated her like a drug. She could be the puppet master, pulling the strings. She laughed and kissed him hard on his lips. "Make an offer. I'll do the rest."

She faithfully performed the rituals, burned the candles, wrapped dollar bills, chanted the prayers, spilled the animal blood. With bare feet, she stepped into the icy Long Island Sound, and she walked in the woods to connect with the spirits. Everything Lourdes suggested, she obeyed. In return, she felt untouchable. She had Jude's love, a baby on the way, and soon she would have a house along the Long Island Sound, a dwelling worthy of Yemayá, the great mother who lived and ruled over fish and seas.

And so, Jude received a raise at not just one hospital, but both. To celebrate closing on their first home, Jude and Isabel ate at Sammy's Fish Box on the Island.

City Island, a small fishing town, was only a half-mile wide. Jude and Isabel walked the length of the island down City Island Avenue. The quaint main street—decorated for Christmas, shaded by elms and dotted with antique shops and seafood restaurants— seemed a world away from the crime, stink, and filth of Manhattan.

Her face felt sore from the cold and from smiling all afternoon. Isabel had spent most of the day imagining what it would feel like to push a stroller down the main street in spring. She pictured the vacant rooms in their soon-to-be home, the large bay windows facing the sound, the brick fireplace, the wood floors. She envisioned the placement for couches, love seats, a dining room table, bar stools, beds, armoires. There was so much shopping to be done before the baby. She planned to sew the curtains herself. Throw pillows, too. She wanted everything ready, wall-papered and decorated.

When Jude and Isabel showed up at closing to sign the mortgage papers, the seller of the house pulled Jude aside. "You didn't say your wife was Black."

"She's not," said Jude. "She's Puerto Rican." He smiled and crossed muscular tattooed arms in front of his chest. "What are you getting at?"

The seller twitched nervously. "We're tight knit around here. I'm a clam digger myself, proud of it. That's what we call locals."

"Oh, yeah." Jude took a toothpick from his shirt pocket and picked at his teeth. "What do you call outsiders?"

"Mussel suckers." The seller grinned and flushed a deeper shade of red.

"I dig it," said Jude. "Enough with the bullshit. We're buying the house."

JUGGERNAUT

Puerto Rico
1950

The year Paula gave birth to her daughter Isabel, Nacionalistas led an uprising in El Oso Blanco Penitentiary, and more than one hundred inmates broke free. The baby in Paula's arms wailed for milk, so she hastily glanced at the front page of *El Imparcial* and read the headline, "*Motín en El Presidio, 110 Se Fugan Tras Matar Guardias.*" She placed the newspaper back on the table to read to Rosendo in the evening, and said a silent prayer for the families of the three guards killed in the prison riot.

She sat in a wooden rocker under the shade of their shack and nursed the six month old as she watched Jacob and Esau chase lizards with tin cans. Joseph, only a few inches taller than the twins and with hair the color of dark honey, stood alone beside the narrow porch, hunched over a pile of fire ants. The ants swarmed around a dragonfly, picking the carcass clean, and Joseph kicked dirt over the small mound with his big toe. "*Tate quieto,*" she snapped at Joseph. She knew fire ants to attack all at once, to spread and sting up the legs in seconds.

Paula thought about the *politicos* who had escaped the prison, the men and women serving time for disobeying the 1948 *Ley de la Mordaza,* and felt a knot twist in the pit of her stomach. The gag laws on the island had criminalized any talk of independence. Whistling "*La Borinqueña*" had become a crime, and owning a Puerto Rican flag a felony against the U.S. government. She thought about Alberto, who could never hold his tongue, yet for thirteen long years, she'd heard no word from him. Was he even alive, or was he rotting somewhere in a prison?

Then on the morning of the prison riot and the fire ants, there he was. It was as if seeing a man risen from a dream, so remarkably changed. He pulled up in a black Plymouth wearing a linen coat, new shoes, and a navy silk tie, looking as if he had walked off the movie screen at Cine Luna. She stood at her front door, eyes stinging, unable to speak or move.

"Mami, who's that man?" Joseph stood waist high, tugging at Paula's housedress. She became aware of her own unshapely *bata*, her *chancleta* slippers, and the eight pregnancies still heavy on her hips and waist.

Paula didn't answer. For a moment, she no longer recognized herself or the boy. She placed a shaky hand on the back of his warm neck to steady herself.

"He's my brother." Rosendo's sharp voice startled her, and she moved from the open door to let him pass between her and the boy. "You both go inside," he said. "I'll see what he wants."

Paula didn't want to pry her eyes away, but she took the boy's reluctant hand and pulled him into the house and called the twins to follow her inside.

"But I want to see the car," said Joseph.

"Not right now," Paula said. "Mind your own business."

"Who's here?" Esau asked.

"What's wrong with you boys? Have I raised a house of busybodies?" she snapped. "No more talking."

Paula walked into a windowless back room and placed the baby in her bassinet. She pressed her palm to her forehead and tried to breathe. A mirror hung above the dresser, and she assessed her reflection, feeling a feverish heat rise to her face. Maybe she was getting sick? She took a deep breath. Beside a vase filled with artificial flowers, she opened a Band-Aid tin and removed several bobby pins. With five pins held between her pursed lips, she used both hands to lift hair off the back of her neck. With quick fingers she coiled black curls into a twist and pinned the knot into place. Fumbling with the buttons of her bata, she stepped out of the housedress and stood in nothing but her slip.

From the table, she heard Jacob's tearful voice. "Mami, Joseph keeps spitting in my food."

"Liar, I did not!" said Joseph.

"You did, too!" said Esau, ever the defender of his twin.

"You boys cut it out this second! Don't make me come over there." The rising shrill of her own voice unsettled her. She felt sweat trickle down her back. She picked up a tin of talc powder and sprinkled it on her chest. Even in her haste, she folded the housedress neatly and placed it in one of the dresser drawers. From the makeshift closet, she pulled her Sunday dress off a hanger and hurried with the zipper. When she was finished dressing, she exchanged her chancletas for more sensible leather flats and looked into the mirror again to pinch her cheeks and smear Vaseline across her mouth.

Joseph sat at the table and sulked. "Where are you going?"

"Nowhere," said Paula. "Now, stop teasing your brothers."

"I didn't do nothing," he said. "Jacob's being a baby."

"He is not," said Esau.

Joseph was sixteen months older than the twins, and normally, Paula would have scolded him for picking on his brothers. Now, she ignored him, her mind racing with questions.

Rosendo stepped through the open Dutch door, his body filling the frame, and met Paula's eyes with a stone expression. "He means to speak to us both."

"*Ay, Dios mio.*" Paula picked up her mug of cold coffee and motioned for the boys to stand. In her nervousness, she almost knocked over one of their chairs.

"What's the matter with you?" said Rosendo.

"Nothing." She cleared the table and placed dishes in a plastic wash bin. She checked her dress to make sure water hadn't splashed on the fabric.

Rosendo sneered. "What, you plan to play me dirty?"

139

"What are you talking about?" she said.

"What's with the dress?"

"Please, don't start. I wasn't decent."

"I call a spade a spade," he said.

"I changed is all."

"For him."

"For me. Please, don't make a scene. Not today."

Before he could reply, Alberto entered their tiny living room, his Panama hat in his hands.

"It's good to see you," he said to Paula, greeting her, kissing her cheek gently in the customary way. She breathed in the citrus and rosemary scent on his skin, the Lucky Tiger smell of hair tonic and aftershave, nothing like the boy she remembered. His dark, intense eyes fixed on Paula, and he smiled a timid smile.

She had imagined their reunion a thousand times before, the questions she would ask, the stories she would tell him. In her fantasies, they were always alone, conveniently in their Sunday best, bumping into one another on the same street at the same time. Calle Sol or Avenida Estevez surrounded by strangers, unencumbered. Now she felt the eyes of Rosendo and her young sons on her back, singeing, hot-coal eyes.

She felt a girlish urge to hide. "Please, have a seat," she said, but he remained standing, glancing around the room.

A cotton sheet hung on a line dividing the kitchen and living room from two back bedrooms, and an overstuffed sofa rested against a bare wall.

"I'm sorry if this is a bad time," he said. His kind tone made her only more nervous. It seemed to wrap around her like a shawl, press in on all sides.

"Don't be silly." She laughed, forcing a smile. "You're family."

She looked away to catch her breath, to hold back tears that kept creeping behind her eyes. The cramped shack felt crowded with the two men hovering over the small table, and the boys shuffling their bare feet on the cement floor, waiting to be noticed.

"These are our youngest boys, Joseph, Jacob, and Esau," said Rosendo. "Boys, say hello to your Tío Alberto."

Alberto crouched to their level, and each boy shook his hand warmly. "Can I get a ride in your car?" said Joseph.

"That's enough," said Rosendo. "Get outside, now. We need to talk."

The boys didn't argue. The children had learned early to regard their father with caution.

"The four oldest left for school already," Rosendo said. "You probably passed them on the road."

"Amazing. Seven beautiful children," said Alberto.

"Eight," Paula corrected him. "The baby is asleep." She gestured to the curtain.

Rosendo scooted the newspaper and AM radio to the corner and sat down in one of the three wooden chairs. Alberto sat beside him and placed his Panama in his lap.

"Can I get you some coffee?" Paula asked.

"No, nothing for me, thank you," said Alberto.

Rosendo waved an agitated hand at her. "Just sit down, for Chrissakes."

She sensed both men's eyes on her face, one irritated, the other pained. She tucked her trembling hands around her waist, afraid to look directly at either man, afraid her eyes would reveal things best forgotten.

"Jesus, man, we haven't seen you since you left for Ponce," said Rosendo. "I thought you were dead."

"Not dead," said Alberto. "I landed in jail for three weeks." He looked down at his feet for a moment, pausing to find the words. "I'm sorry," he said. "God, I'm so sorry. I knew this wouldn't be easy, but now that I'm here, it's damn near impossible." He lit a cigarette, exhaled and offered a drag to Rosendo. "Like old times," he said.

Rosendo nodded thanks and blew smoke from the corner of his mouth, his eyes never leaving Alberto's face. "You look just the same, ugly as hell."

Alberto laughed weakly to himself.

Rosendo offered the cigarette back to Alberto, but he waved it away. "So. Explain how three weeks turned into ten years."

"Thirteen," said Paula quietly. "Start at the beginning. Tell us everything."

Alberto took a deep breath before he spoke. "Ponce." He let the word out like a sigh. "The police shot us down in the streets."

"We know all that," Rosendo interrupted. "Tell us what we don't know."

"After that, they went to the hospitals and rounded up wounded cadets to make more arrests. All I remember is being clubbed in the back of the head. Next thing I knew, the police were handcuffing me right off my stretcher. They locked me up for three weeks on trumped-up charges."

"Why would they arrest you?" Paula sensed Rosendo's annoyance. He was the man, and she should let him ask the questions, but she had waited far too long for answers. The words slipped out, unrestrained.

"For sedition," said Alberto. "That's when I put it together. It was like my eyes were open for the first time, and I realized diplomacy would fail. The system was rigged, just like Albizu Campos had always said it was, designed to enslave us. I saw it with my own eyes."

"Rigged?" Paula repeated the word to herself, felt it crumble over and over again in her mind. She thought of Alberto, not the sophisticated man sitting in her kitchen, but the country boy she once knew, lying on the floor of a prison, his head still oozing with blood. She wanted to reach her hand across the table, to say something to comfort him, but she had no words. With Rosendo beside her, she tried to make her face unreadable. She clasped her hands tightly in her lap, and stared down at the table. She felt like she would crack in two.

"When I was released on bail from La Princesa, I was in bad shape with a fever, not to mention flat broke. The gash on my head was infected, and I didn't get far. I collapsed on the side of the road. Then two men carried me in a hammock straight back to the hospital. Nurses said I was there a few weeks, but they saved my life."

Rosendo leaned forward in his chair. "Always the lucky bastard."

"When I recovered, I took a job near the docks to scrape together some money. I managed to call a friend of Mamá's, a neighbor with a telephone, and I left word that I was okay. But after all I'd seen in Ponce and in La Princessa, I just couldn't . . . I couldn't find my way back to normal. I was so angry. I couldn't think about nothing else. A little after that, Mamá arranged to call me back. That's when I heard about your marriage." He glanced up at Rosendo, who met his steady gaze through a cloud of smoke. "You're the lucky one."

Paula flushed. "Your mother never said a word to us. She never told us you had contacted her, never said you were all right. Why wouldn't she have told us?"

"You want a drink?" said Rosendo. Without giving Alberto time to respond, Rosendo told Paula to bring the bottle of whiskey from the cabinet along with two clean glasses.

Paula stood, weak-kneed, trying to puzzle together the pieces of Alberto's story. All these years, doña Carmen had known where he was, and she had said nothing. Before she had a chance to set the glasses on the table, she heard the baby cry from the bedroom. Paula set the bottle of whiskey on the table and retreated behind the curtain.

As she began to nurse the baby, she could hear Rosendo pouring generously into each glass. "*Salud,*" he said.

She heard the clinking of two glasses and Alberto saying, "To family."

When she returned to the room with a tear-streaked baby, their glasses were empty.

"Little savages," Rosendo said. "All they do is eat, sleep, and crap."

"Who's this little doll?" Alberto waved at the baby, and she tucked her face into her mother's neck.

Paula balanced the baby on one hip. "Our youngest, Isabel. Please, won't you tell us the rest?"

"Things were happening fast in those days. With Albizu Campos in a federal prison, it was nearly impossible to keep recruits. Everyone was scared, but the time was ripe to organize. The blood of the Ponce martyrs was still fresh on the streets. By then, there were only a few hundred of us cadets left, but we ran up and down Monte de Hatillo performing drills."

"What the hell for?" said Rosendo.

Alberto stared at him with quiet desperation. "Because they gunned down women and children. After that, I couldn't sit back and do nothing. In prison, I had made connections, and I worked my way up among the cadets. During the war, I took a job on a ship that sailed for months at a time to France. I made money on the side selling contraband, cigarette cartons, chocolate bars, stuff like that. When the war ended, I kept at it. Now I organize shipments for the Nationalists."

Paula looked up from the table and saw his eyes were far away as he spoke. "What kind of shipments?"

Rosendo shot her a sharp look. "Would you let the man talk?"

"I'm doing whatever I can to help the cause." Alberto said the words slowly, letting the weight of his meaning settle before he spoke again. His eyes shifted between Paula and Rosendo. Rosendo scooted his chair closer to Paula and rested a possessive arm on the back of her chair. She stiffened.

"The shipments come off the docks out of Santurce," Alberto said, "and I have safe houses all over the island."

"You mean guns?" Rosendo said.

Alberto nodded quietly.

"Why are you telling us this?" Paula didn't want to hear anymore. His words alone put them all at risk. "I think maybe you should leave."

"Please," he said, his expression an apology. "I wouldn't have come, but everything is about to change. Vidal Santiago, an important captain, has gone missing. He runs a barber shop in Santurce where we stash supplies, but a few weeks ago, he vanished. Now the place is surrounded by the FBI. I can't go near it."

"What does any of this have to do with us?" she said.

"I need a safe place to hide several crates until I can find out what's happened to Vidal."

"No way," said Rosendo. "Absolutely not. Take your crates to another one of your houses. We got enough troubles, we don't need yours."

"Please, brother. I wouldn't have come if I had another choice. We think there's a snitch. Informants among the Nationalists. Maybe spies at the highest levels, but until I know for sure, there is no one else I can trust with these boxes. I think they've got Vidal locked up in Aguadilla. Men I knew from La Princesa say there's a place near the airport, a place where Nationalists are taken to be tortured. Vidal is the personal barber of Pedro Albizu Campos, among his closest advisers. If Vidal cracks, it's over."

"And this is why you've come?" said Paula. "For this?" She couldn't hide the pained expression on her face. He hadn't come for her after all. "No, we won't do it. Find someone else."

"I came because I trust you," he said. "More than anyone in the world." He looked at her sincerely for a long moment and turned to Rosendo. "With Mamá gone, you and Paula are the only family I have left."

"How long?" said Rosendo.

"Just for a couple of weeks. I can't keep these crates in the trunk of my car. They're searching cars."

"What if they search the house?" she said.

"Why would they? You have no connection to the Party. The police would have no reason to suspect—"

"We have eight children, Alberto," said Paula. "Babies. You can't expect—"

"I know," he said. "I would never intentionally bring harm to your family, but I need help."

"And where were you when Mamá died?" Rosendo said. "Where were you when we needed help to put food on this table?" Paula knew that Rosendo had waited a long time to say those words to his brother, and she could see the smug expression on his face as he spoke.

"I told you." Alberto's grieved expression sent a fresh wave of pain through Paula.

"Oh, yeah, that's right," said Rosendo. "You've been too busy fighting Yankee occupation."

"You have every right to be angry." Alberto's eyes were sorrowful. "But I didn't abandon our mother. I sent her money when I could. How do you think I knew how to find you?"

Paula positioned the baby over her shoulder and patted her back. "You let us believe the worst. Surely, you could have written."

"I thought it would be easier if I didn't."

"Easier for you." There was bitterness in her words, and she instantly regretted speaking.

"Mamá thought it would be best for the family, for everyone, if I stayed away. She knew my commitment to the struggle."

Paula noticed him look nervously out the window a second time. "I know it's hard for you to understand."

"Bullshit," said Rosendo. "You don't care about this family. You never did. Otherwise, you wouldn't be here now, asking us to put our necks on the line."

"It's not like that."

"You tell me then. What *is* it like, baby brother?"

"I promise you, it's just for a short time, until I can know for sure it's safe to move the crates into the city, until I can speak with Vidal."

"If I do this, what's in it for me?" Rosendo asked.

"Money," said Alberto. "Enough money to get your family out of here, to start a new life."

Rosendo rubbed the back of his neck. He looked at Paula, who quietly shook her head, no. "It's too dangerous," she said.

Her husband rubbed a dirty fingernail across his bottom lip and slouched deeper into his chair. "Two weeks," he said. "You have two weeks to find another place."

*

Violence was in the air. In town, people guarded their words. They whispered like *bandidos* and took to looking over their shoulders even on their front porches. The *carpetas*, the secret police dossiers recording the personal lives of teachers, professors, journalists, and businessmen suspected of supporting Puerto Rican independence, were widely known. Political newspapers criticized the carpetas openly, but it didn't stop the government from imprisoning and destroying the careers of anyone who found their name on a list of subversives. Had Alberto told anyone about the crates under their house? She didn't want to know what was inside, but she suspected it was enough to get her name on one of the carpetas, enough to make a person disappear.

As she waited for Alberto to return, Paula couldn't help but think about the disappeared, the barber Vidal, and the other Nationalists who seemed to vanish right off the streets. She found it impossible not to think of him. She tried not to think of him in the damp, early mornings when the chickens peeped around her ankles. She tried not to think of him when she looked into the dim eyes of her eight children. She told herself, *You are in love with a ghost. He is not the same schoolboy holding your hand under a gaslight in the plaza, and you are not that girl.* The day of the Ponce Massacre had changed all that, not only for him but for her as well. He lived only for independence, and she lived for her children.

Her body told the story of each birth in stretched skin, swollen hands, and legs that throbbed under varicose veins. At thirty years old, she felt ancient. Her body was not her own.

Rosendo emerged from their wooden shack and sat in the open doorway, shaded by the overhanging tin roof. He wore only loose-fitting trousers, and Paula noticed gray hairs flecking his broad chest. "I need to get out of here," he said, watching Paula adjust the baby against her engorged breast. He had been listening to WIAC radio all morning, cursing and pacing back and forth in the tiny living room. She knew to stay out of his way. Juanita helped with the baby, but she had sent Angel to sell *quenepa* fruit and the older girls to the *tienda* to buy toothpaste, milk, and a pack of Lucky Strikes for their papi. "They've already arrested four hundred Nationalists. The radio said there might be a thousand more arrests by the end of the week."

"What are you talking about?"

"Police surrounded a farmhouse suspected of hiding guns in Peñuelas. Everyone inside was either killed or arrested."

"Lord have mercy." Paula called their twelve-year-old, Juanita, from her needlework and handed the baby to the girl to take back into the house.

"They're arresting anyone suspected to be with the Party," he said.

"But how can they do that?"

"Because the world doesn't give a damn what happens here! We're nothing to them."

"What about the girls and Angel? I sent them to town this morning. They shouldn't be in the streets."

"I'll go and get them," he said. "I don't want them out today. Nacionalistas are fighting with the police, burning down post offices and police headquarters all across the island."

"God, help us."

"That's not all. Assassins from Jayuya just tried to kill President Truman in Washington."

"What? This can't be happening."

"Listen to the radio yourself, woman. In Utuado, Ponce, Mayagüez, Arecibo . . . it's chaos. Even the governor's mansion in San Juan was attacked." Rosendo stood to his feet, agitated. "The governor declared martial law."

Paula remembered the last time martial law had been declared on the island. It had been after the Río Piedras massacre that killed four students, after the funeral for Hiram Rosado and Elías Beauchamp and the first arrest of Pedro Albizu Campos. Police broke into homes without warrants. *Los desaparecidos,* the disappeared, all vanished. People were taken away and never heard from again. People like Alberto. People like herself. The horrific thought of her own house surrounded in the dead of night clouded whatever else Rosendo was saying. All she could hear was the imaginary sound of bullets tearing through wood, windows, flesh.

Rosendo turned back into the house, where she could hear him rustling through dresser drawers.

She stood and followed him inside. "What are you doing?"

He pulled at the curtain draped over the clothesline dividing the front room from the back bedrooms, and the baby began to wail from behind the curtain.

"Quiet that baby!" Paula barked her words at Juanita. The girl had anticipated her mother's wishes and had already risen from the table where the radio blared its miserable reports. Juanita slipped behind the curtain to sooth the infant.

"Where are you going?" Paula said. "You'll come right back with the children, right?" She knew to keep the suspicion out of her tone, to soften the question so as not to become the target of his rage.

"I'll send them back," he said, lacing his leather shoes. "I can't just sit here and listen to this play-by-play. I need to find out about Alberto. If it's really revolution, someone is going to come looking for those crates. You expect me to do nothing?"

He buttoned his shirt feverishly, missing one of the buttons. From a high shelf, he grabbed his pocketknife. It wasn't much of a weapon with its two-and-a-half inch blade and corkscrew, but he rarely left the house without it. She approached him cautiously, and with trembling hands she refastened each of his buttons.

"*Dios te bendiga,*" she said.

He didn't answer. His lips twisted in a strange, sad smile. He turned to look at her, and for a moment, they studied each other's familiar faces in bemused silence. Several years earlier, after the war in Europe, she had read a newspaper report about Polish Jews, enslaved prisoners so desperately starved in camps that they had killed one another for a scrap of bread. Sons against fathers, brother against brother. For a moment, she could imagine herself trapped, suffocating among those prisoners. She could see herself, all of them, Alberto, Rosendo, even the children, tearing each other apart, and she felt afraid.

She didn't watch him storm out of the house dressed in his Sunday clothes, the pocket knife still gripped in his fist, but she heard her three boys shout after him, "Papi, where are you going? Papi, take us with you!"

In the distance, she could hear a man on his horse selling baby pigs. She heard the *clip-clop* of the horse's hooves, the man's cracked voice yelling to the cluster of patchwork houses lining the dirt lane. *Lechones, lechones.* She could hear the childlike squeals of the pigs, the shouts of her sons, the wail of the baby, and the sharp, clipped voice on the radio. She heard everything all at once and nothing at all, a fearsome uprising of sound.

She wiped at the tears on her cheek. She considered the possibilities. She was a practical woman, and she refused to submit to hysterics. She wouldn't be the first or the last widow on the island. *God, your will be done*, she prayed. *On Heaven and on Earth.*

She had lain awake plenty of times, wondering if Rosendo would return home after another bout of drinking. The roosters crowed, and the Atlantic waves crashed against the rocky coastline, but beside her, the bed would lie empty. She suspected he pawed on other women, maybe had someone special on the side. Whatever happens, happens, she told herself.

In order to focus her energy on things she could change, she cleaned. She changed the baby's cloth diaper, hand scrubbed the linens in the wash bin, and hung the damp clothes on the line beside the house. She gave each of her three boys a bucket and insisted they help her gather the mango pits, watermelon rinds, and chewed sugarcane stalks from the yard. Downwind from their home, they gathered a pile of food trash and cardboard to burn. They dumped the pile inside a steel, fifty-five-gallon drum, covered the open drum head with a metal grate, and ignited the garbage.

Angel returned home first from a slow day of selling *quenepas* along the side of the road leading to San Juan. Across his shoulders, he carried a cross made of two thick branches, and from the cross, the fruit hung in batches in neat rows. His blue trousers were covered in dust, and his face looked a rosy chestnut color from the heat.

Before entering, he leaned his cross against the house and secured the base with several stones. He washed his hands and face from an outdoor spigot, gulping down mouthfuls of water as he went. Many neighbors still lived without running water or electricity, and Angel felt proud knowing his fruit sales contributed to their family.

Jacob, Esau, and Joseph followed him inside, tracking mud on the wood floor, but Paula swatted them back out the door. "No, you don't. All of you out! You're a mess."

Angel sat at the table and turned on the radio.

"Did you see your papi in town?" Paula lowered the radio volume and poured the boy a cup of coffee.

"I saw him on the road," he said, running a hand through his damp hair. "He told me to get straight home."

She placed a slice of cassava bread on a small ceramic dish, and sat beside him. His eyes, the pale green of a *coquí* underbelly, reminded her of Rosendo's eyes, and like his father, he picked at the bread with his fingers before biting into its soft center.

"I'm glad to see you've got your appetite back," she said.

Several months earlier, Angel had returned home frail and yellow-skinned from the tent hospital where he had been treated for hookworm.

"Papi went to the revolution," Juanita said smugly, excited to possess news her brother knew nothing about. She stood beside the table, bouncing the infant in her arms.

"*Bonchinche*, such a little gossip," Paula scolded. "Nobody's talking to you. Why are you standing around always listening to other people's business? Didn't I already tell you for the tenth time to put that baby down and get your brothers cleaned up?"

Juanita sighed and tried to pry the baby's fingers out of her long, dark curls. "The whole town of Jayuya is on fire," she said as she placed the baby in the bassinet.

"That's enough," said Paula.

"Is it true? Everyone's talking about it on the road." Angel looked nervously between his mother and sister.

"There's been reports all day on the radio. Nationalists are clashing with police again, and Governor Marín called in five thousand National Guardsmen," said Paula.

151

"Someone even tried to kill the president," Juanita said.

"Not another word," said Paula reaching for the slipper on her right foot. She raised the plush slipper in her fist, threatening the girl. "You want a *chanclaso?*"

"Okay, okay," Juanita giggled nervously. "I'm going." She bounced out the door, looking energized by all the fascinating news of fires and assassins.

Celia and Rosa returned with only half the items Paula had requested, but Rosendo remained in town. Paula and her children huddled around the radio for the rest of the afternoon, piecing together the details. In the centrally located mountain city of Jayuya, a young woman named Blanca Canales had led Nacionalistas to surround and attack the police headquarters. They cut the telephone lines and burned the U.S. Post Office before the police surrendered and abandoned the precinct. Freedom fighters, supported by the people of Jayuya, had raised the Puerto Rican flag over the town square, and Blanca Canales had declared the independence of the Republic of Puerto Rico. She shouted to the crowd, "*¡Que viva Puerto Rico libre!*"

In response to the attack on the governor's mansion, *La Fortaleza*, police stormed the Nationalist headquarters with tear gas and arrested Pedro Albizu Campos for the second time.

President Truman sent a P-47 Thunderbolt to bomb the cities of Jayuya and Utuado. Flown by the U.S. National Guard, the Thunderbolt was nicknamed Juggernaut. Its belly-mounted turbochargers, eight .50-caliber machine guns, and 500-pound bombs gunned down almost every tin rooftop. They used the ground-attack aircraft to destroy the fields of the two small towns.

"Mami, why are they doing this?" Angel said when he heard the news. He had spent every waking moment fixated on the radio since returning home.

Paula let his words float in the air between them before answering. "I don't know," she said. "I stopped asking why a long time ago."

"I hate them." He clenched his fists, and a caged expression darkened his broad face.

Celia sat cross-legged at Rosa's feet, while Rosa sat in a chair with a wiry brush combing through her sister's thicket of hair. "You shouldn't hate," Rosa said. "There is no *them*. They are us. We are them. We're Americans, too."

"Not to them," he said. "Not to me."

"Oye, don't argue," said Celia. "Men do what they're gonna do. You can't stop them."

"Like kings?" said Rosa.

"No, like gods." Paula rose from the table, tired of the radio and the children's bickering. "You girls hurry up already, and go fetch water for the barrel." She stepped outside where she collected the laundry from the lines. One by one she folded the clothes and placed them in the large wicker basket at her feet.

A new life. Alberto offered Rosendo a new life, and without hesitation, Rosendo had placed their family on the altar. No one even bothered to ask her what she had wanted, and now both men were gone. *What do you want?* Paula unclipped a pair of men's trousers from the line, and waited for the answer to surface from some deep, unrecognizable well. Empty silence. She could arrange the clothes, but not her own cluttered mind. Her children's faces floated to the surface, and then one by one drifted out of reach. She felt powerless to protect them. It felt simpler to want unmiraculous things, simple things, like a garden to grow sweet potatoes and *yautía*.

She remembered aimless days as a girl knocking coconuts from branches beside a country house painted butter yellow, her mother's almond trees and breadfruit growing in the yard. Was she ever so young? Maybe all of it, every breath, the babies, youth, maybe all of it was miraculous. If it was, the men were tearing it all apart inch by inch.

In the Psalms, she'd read that the heavens declared the glory of God; the skies proclaimed the work of his hands. She looked up into the clear sky, half expecting to see a warplane on the horizon or Jesus himself on a cloud. Day after day the skies poured forth speech. Words were on the radio, on the lips of her neighbors, the fighting words of her husband, but those were the wrong words. In the beginning was the word, and there were words to the ends of the earth. In a single word God spoke light and it manifested. Everyone and everything started as a word, so why couldn't she think of a single word to say what she wanted? All she could think of were the thousand little things she didn't want. She didn't want another hurricane. She didn't want Rosendo to stumble home drunk looking for an excuse to slap her good. She didn't want illness or death to spring upon her children. But most of all, she didn't want to wake another day with Rosendo's hands grabbing at her breasts, prying her legs apart. She didn't want Alberto to come back, stirring up memories of the boy she had tried so hard to forget. Then it came to her, a singular thing to want, and the thought made her ashamed—a world without men.

CRYSTAL BALL

1985

The year she turned ten, Esther and her mother vacationed in St. Thomas, and that spring break, Esther's nose and cheeks peeled the pale peach of a conch's innards. Standing on a chair in the hotel bathroom, she leaned against the porcelain sink and studied her face in the mirror as she lifted veils of translucent skin with the tips of her fingers. She let the flakes settle on the counter and admired her new, exposed face.

Two decades later, no amount of whitening creams, glycolic peels, or microderms would erase the dark spots that would rise to the surface of her skin like islands, reminding her of the damage of that tropical sun and a man named Daniel.

Her mother met Daniel poolside at the waterfront hotel. She was in a red string bikini and her oiled skin had slicked and baked to a warm sienna bronze. He had a forty-foot performance motorsailer that could go up to fourteen knots, *Top Gun* aviator lenses, and a know-it-all smile.

In those days, her mother was spontaneous, bullish with her will. Unafraid. At thirty-five, she had a combination of sensuality and bewitching confidence that made her pulse with energy. Esther noticed men notice her mother. She saw them look away at first, as if singed by a burning coal, then track her mother's movements from the corners of their eyes.

After witnessing years of their loveless marriage, it didn't surprise Esther that her mother had flirted her way onto Daniel's boat, but it did surprise her that she'd been left behind, alone at the hotel. All afternoon, two chalky boys cannonballed into the pool. They splashed Esther on purpose, and her skin pruned and burned. Later that evening, her mother introduced her to Daniel. He ordered chocolate ice cream from the pool attendant and gave Esther a pearly shell pinched out of the Caribbean. At dinner, Daniel joined them, and her mother drank too much wine and giggled in an unrecognizably girlish way. Esther sipped from a virgin piña colada with a colorful parasol garnish while a calypso drummer's steely *taca taca* pulsated in the torchlight of the restaurant.

For the rest of the week, Daniel became their private tour guide. He owned a vacation home on nearby St. John, and he said he knew the island better than the locals. Esther didn't say anything when her mother tucked her wedding ring into her makeup bag, but she dreaded the lies she'd have to tell her father and her friends back home. Without needing an explanation, Esther understood the powerful spell of a man's singular attention. It was no secret. Her mother felt neglected by her father, and for this, too, Esther blamed him. What was the harm? Daniel, like all things on their vacation, was supposed to be temporary. That was the intention, anyway, for him to be nothing more than a fleeting snapshot, something forgotten and sealed away in an album behind sticky transparent covers.

Rules didn't apply to Daniel. He drove the wrong way down the one-way cobblestone streets, laughing like a madman, which made her mother laugh till tears rolled down her cheeks. He boasted that he knew all the shortcuts on the island, the best markets for jewelry, the best reefs for snorkeling.

She didn't want to be the keeper of her mother's secrets, a witness to her deception. More than a witness, by accepting Daniel's token gifts and laughing at his jokes and admiring the ways he seemed to outshine her father, she felt like a cheater herself. She was no daddy's girl, and that acknowledgment broke her heart. So, Esther justified and collaborated in her mother's affair by saying nothing to stop it.

*

In the MTV video of "Material Girl," Madonna dressed like the bombshell Marilyn Monroe and reenacted "Diamonds are a Girl's Best Friend." In her rendition, Madonna offered her unwanted diamond necklace to a friend on the phone and drove off with the man of her dreams in an old, beat-up truck. In his hands, he held daisies instead of diamonds. And there was Madonna in her hot-pink gown and her lush fur wrap. Esther didn't like the song and pressed fast forward on her Walkman every time it played, but she found the video mesmerizing. There on the TV screen was unapologetic femininity and sexuality on full display. So brazen, so like her mother. She desperately wanted to believe in her mother's innocence. In her own innocence.

Back home, Esther and her friends dialed 1-900 numbers to learn about sex. The automated messages were a forbidden language, and little by little, Esther tried to piece together the unknowable bits of her good-girl self and her body.

She locked herself in her room and picked at the skin around her nails until her fingers and toes throbbed and bled.

Then in the summer before middle school, in the middle of her mother's emotional breakdown, Esther's parents divorced. The divorce hadn't come as a surprise to anyone, especially not Esther, but leaving her home and friends in City Island and moving with her mother to Puerto Rico came as a complete shock.

Feeling raw, it was there in Puerto Rico where Esther first met her great-uncle, Tío Maximo, and his mind reading wife. It was early September, but in Puerto Rico, even the morning sun baked the car's interior. On the bench seat of the yellow Lincoln Town Car, hot, cracked vinyl burned branches across the backs of Esther's exposed thighs. She sat invisibly still between her driver, Tío Maximo, and his wife, who now drove her each morning to a new, all-English private school on the east side of the island.

Three miles into their first drive together, Esther sensed the wife's eyes resting on her bare knees. Without moving her neck, she knew the woman's feather gaze brushed her narrow hips, skimmed up her scrawny arms, and probed her innermost flat-chested thoughts.

Esther tucked her school uniform tighter around her legs. She settled into the warm seat and tried her best not to think. Tío Maximo's wife sat in a floral housedress, hogging the passenger window and the fresh air blowing in from the street. The loose dress muted her body, and her coarse white hair was tied back in a bun above her neck. Her legs were dry and scaled, peeling birch knees and spindly calves that crossed at her ankles. Her feet were two pink nylon slippers. Her hands rested on her lap, and Esther couldn't help notice the woman's way of stroking the back of one hand with the tips of her fingers, petting a bulging vein as if it were a kitten.

With her backpack at her feet, Tío Maximo on the driver's side, and Tía Whatshername on the passenger's side, Esther felt hemmed in, trapped. She sat shoulder to bony shoulder, feeling the sweat slip down the back of her uniform and Tía quietly peeking into her mind. The woman was slow at first, stealthy. With the furtive movements of a thief, she tiptoed into her thoughts and flipped the private pages. Esther imagined her licking the tips of her cracked fingers before turning to the next memory. She gazed out the windshield as a flush of humiliation rose to her cheeks. Years later, as a young woman, her first awkward visit to the gynecologist would remind her of those helpless commutes to and from the English academy. Tía the Mind Reader, like the good doctor, strapping her in and prying her open.

Her only defense against her great-aunt was a mental barricade. So, on her morning commute, she mentally recited tongue twisters until she was dropped off at the academy's gates. She locked her thoughts on Peter Piper and pushed the words to the surface of her mind like a shield.

Peter Piper picked a peck of pickled peppers
Peter Piper picked a peck of pickled peppers…

In Puerto Rico, her family called her *la gringa* because she took ballet lessons and didn't know the difference between a salsa or a merengue. She preferred take-out Chinese, bagels, pizza slices, burgers, spaghetti, and chicken nuggets, and wrinkled her nose at beans, both red and black. She refused to eat food drizzled with pique sauce, and didn't even like her Titi Celia's renowned bread pudding. They called her *flaquita,* skin and bones.

Tío Maximo, her grandmother's oldest brother, was also all bones. He stood soldier straight, and each morning, he arrived precisely at seven forty-five to drive her to school. He waited for her at the curb with the heavy driver's door open, and as she slouched toward him, she felt like a sullen turtle in her green plaid uniform and bulging backpack.

Esther didn't make a single friend at the academy. Her time there felt like a performance. The school uniform, a costume. The tropical paradise, a set. To make things worse, she couldn't seem to remember any of her lines since they were all in Spanish. Much to her distress, she couldn't roll her *R*s or conjugate verbs. She tried not to say anything beyond basic greetings, mumbling barely audible words that felt thick and sticky over her braces.

With her hair cinched into a Cyndi Lauper banana clip, her ponytail bobbed and spasmed each time the car rolled over one of Fajardo's many potholes. Tío Maximo had to be alert, shifting around broken pavement, dodging the wild dogs. In the rainy season, the streets would flood.

The ride to school was only twenty minutes, but Esther sat in white-knuckled silence while Tío Maximo hummed *jibaro* mountain songs. He turned up the radio and drummed on the steering wheel with his calloused thumbs. Sometimes the songs slipped into melancholic melodies, full of longing and desire, and Esther thought of home on the Long Island Sound. Then her thoughts would unravel like fishing line, and she would let the lure fly. Images of City Island with its long stretches of sand. Seafood shacks and the smell of fried shrimp. Marinas and the lulling sound of buoys clinking off metal, the call of the seagulls, the autumn leaves igniting with color in her backyard a thousand miles away. Then, like a kick to the gut, she would think of her closest friends, heading off to middle school without her. Her throat closed, and all these thoughts were cast out before she remembered the mind reader. She bit the inside of her cheek. She focused on the sensation of pain and with a steel focus reeled back the unguarded thoughts, inch by inch, out of her Tía's reach.

She returned to *Peter Piper picked a peck of pickled peppers,* while Tío Maximo's wife sat beside her pretending not to notice. It was exhausting, this mental barricade, and by the time she arrived at school, she was so relieved to have her thoughts back to herself, that she didn't even mind that the building smelled of mold or that some of the boys called her *Come mierda* behind her back. She seemed impervious to the girls who cut their eyes at her with long mascara lashes and huddled their desks into tight whispering circles, leaving her out of their secrets.

At recess, she hid in the musty library, which was the size of a bathroom stall. The boys were on the prowl for bra straps, and since she had no straps to pull, this was a tiny mortification she did her best to avoid.

Even so, school was better than being trapped in the car with the mind reader or at home with her mother. At least in the tiny library, she had the freedom to peruse the ancient-looking, leather-bound books. There was no librarian, no card catalog, only a heavy wooden table with empty seats. The window with its chipped shutters swung open, facing the busy town plaza. The books with their yellowing pages lined the walls, left to rot. Each day, she shoved one into her backpack to take home and rescue.

One slim paperback entitled *Songs of Madness and Other Poems* by Francisco Matos Paoli caught her attention because it had a peculiar dedication: "To Lolita Lebrón, our Joan of Arc." Esther had heard of the Roman Catholic saint, a French martyr burned at the stake, but who was this Lolita? Although the book wasn't hers to mark, with a pencil she underlined a line that seemed to pop from the pages. *Why do I disappear?*

Before she could finish the poem, she heard the click of señora Guzman's heels in the hall. She shoved the slim book up her uniform romper and wrapped her arms around her chest, pressing the paperback close to her stomach.

Later that night in her bed, she read more curious lines from Paoli's poetry: "The Leader's name is Pedro. / Rock of Puerto Rico, fluvial and winged Rock / with aroma of martyred blood / from Palm Sunday." She flipped to the back of the book where she read about Pedro Albizu Campos, the Palm Sunday Massacre, and the Nobel Prize-nominated poet Paoli, imprisoned for insurrection during the 1950 revolution.

Esther couldn't figure it out. What revolution? She'd taken Puerto Rican history in the seventh grade and had never heard of any of these people. Disconnected from the island's history, the lines in the poem reminded her instead of the U2 song "Sunday Bloody Sunday." She'd watched the band perform the song during Live Aid as images of starving children with bloated bellies filled her television screen.

She'd heard of political prisoners like Nelson Mandela, but never had she heard of Pedro Albizu Campos, who had suffered radiation torture while serving time in a federal prison, or the poet Paoli who went mad in prison after years of solitary confinement and electric shock therapy. Here was an alternative history, so unfamiliar. Like the disappeared.

*

The crystal ball, the size of a child's skull, appeared out of place in Esther's sitting room. It was a room suited for old white women, wearing prim white gloves. A room decorated for tea parties, Victorians, and chilled champagne; an impractical room in Puerto Rico. Impractical anywhere.

Her mother studied the crystal ball, her expression somber and serious. Esther hardly recognized her, and she had no idea what her mother was doing, no idea what unspeakable things she could possibly see inside the glass. With each passing year, her mother had grown more sullen, more agitated, fluctuating from manic highs to dark depression.

Her mother peered into the crystal ball like the gypsy fortune-teller of a thousand movie scenes. Esther had never seen her like this before, so focused, with her clairvoyant power directed on the crystal and on her.

"I am very disappointed in you, young lady." The shadows under her mother's eyes and around her mouth deepened. She sounded ancient, strained.

"I haven't done anything wrong." Esther shifted in her seat and felt as if she were about to cry. Maybe she was crying already. Her mother's words stung worse than any sucker punch to the gut. Esther did everything to please her. She was a classic goody-goody, teacher's pet, with straight As and no drinking, no drugs, no making out with boys. "I'm a good girl," she mumbled.

Her mother had never subjected her to this type of interrogation before. Esther couldn't see anything in the crystal ball, but apparently whatever her mother saw made her scoff at the girl's words. Her mother's full lips turned to hard lines, her eyes scowled.

"You think you can just sneak around behind my back? Do you think I'm stupid?"

Esther had heard these words many times before, but always, they'd been reserved for her father. "No." Esther's voice sounded weak. Her mother could crush her in an instant.

"I won't tolerate lying," her mother snapped.

"I know."

"God, I've had about enough of this family. It's bad enough I had to deal with your father, but now you, too?"

"I'm sorry," Esther whimpered. "What did I do?"

"You know exactly what you did. Don't play dumb."

Esther's mind buzzed. She ransacked her memory for anything she could have done to upset her mother.

"My *Egun* tells me everything. Don't you know that by now?"

Esther let the words sink in. The thought solidified in her head. It gnawed at her edges. Her mother's father, her spirit guide, watched over them, always over her shoulder like some invisible tattletale. Her mind raced: Mrs. Rodriguez catching her slip a note in class, the cheat sheet someone handed her before science. The time Luis dropped his pants on the back of the bus during a field trip. The time at recess when Carlos put his knees on her chest and spread his tongue up the side of her cheek in one slimy sweep. What else had he seen? Esther shuddered.

She imagined her mother's Watcher watching, and as her mind swallowed the stones of her mother's words, Esther felt him. In that moment, right there on the Victorian love seats, she felt his eyes on her. Hadn't she always felt them? Hadn't she always known? She felt his smug presence saying there was nowhere to hide.

Her mother took a drag from a thick cigar, puffing clouds of smoke toward the crystal globe. The smoke coiled serpentine around the glass.

Esther stared at the ground, silenced. She didn't speak or defend herself further as her mother berated her for her secrets. Every ounce of fight sapped out of the girl. Esther just wanted to be left alone. *Never alone*, she felt the Watcher say.

Her mother's voice rattled the fragile porcelain in its glass cases, and Esther felt her insides melt into puddles.

When it was over, she nodded in surrender.

"You can't lie to me, Esther. You understand me? Get that through your thick skull. I see everything."

Once, Esther saw a movie about a diseased boy who lived inside a bubble to stay alive. She remembered next to nothing about the film, but sometimes when her parents argued or her mother wept for reasons she refused to explain, Esther felt the clear, thin bubble wrap around her, too. There, inside the bubble, she went completely numb. No amount of yelling or tears could touch her.

"Go to your room," her mother said through the bubble's shield. "I don't want to even see your face."

Shame is all eyes. Teeth. Shame is the peeping tom, his binoculars at the window frame. Shame is the forever Watcher, crouching in Esther's corners.

Esther retreated to her room and pressed a pillow to her face. She stared at the unlocked door, wondering if she could sense the moment the Watcher entered, a specter that guarded and lurked. She listened for him to slip through the keyhole, waited for his invisible touch to rest on the back of her neck.

After that, her mother didn't speak again about the crystal ball. And Esther didn't ask about the glasses of water, the coins, and the flowers her mother exchanged for Esther's secrets.

The very next morning, while brushing her teeth, Esther felt a presence slide up beside her in the bathroom. Panic rushed her hand as she scrubbed the toothbrush over her braces. She didn't look into the mirror over the sink, horrified of what she might see behind her. She didn't want to see the ghostly figure, not ever. Mirrors, reflections, still waters—all held a looming presence, a presence that morphed into twisted faces. She couldn't stop seeing them. She was surrounded.

As Esther walked out the front door, she resisted looking in the direction of the waifish specters who balanced on the iron fence. Sharp, angular creatures gargoyled off tile rooftops. They dangled from streetlamps. No matter how hard she tried, she couldn't stop seeing them. Maybe she was going crazy? She didn't say a word to anyone. In her classroom, they crammed under desks, paraded down hallways, sat cross-legged on bookshelves.

No part of herself remained hidden. She gave up. She submitted completely to her mother's powers. She chased perfection. She picked raw skin bloody. She plucked the hairs from her legs with tweezers, one by one. She locked and relocked bathroom doors. She tried to look quickly past the eyes in her windows, to ignore the hands that reached through the walls, the grabs for her ankles from under the bed. She had solidified her faith in her mother's spirits and in her magic. She had no doubt in her mother's abilities. Fear and compulsion became her touchstone and her moral compass, guiding her toward sainthood.

By the time she graduated, the students at the high school had given her a new nickname—the nun.

164

OMENS

Each night as Isabel fell asleep, a chatter of voices rose from the silence. Sometimes she heard her name spoken in the dark, a knock at the door, signs of her *Egun* calling. Lately, she dreamed warning dreams. Sirens rang off in her mind. Images of ominous clouds, dark waters, falling stars, home invaders, consuming fires. Bad omens. She envisioned Esther bound by thick ropes, tied in tight, hard knots. She combed through dream interpretation books searching the symbols.

Back in City Island, a friend had suggested she see a therapist to deal with her childhood traumas. The psychologist, a freckled woman with wire-rimmed glasses, a double chin, and twenty-five years of experience, said, "It's called auditory hallucinations," and Isabel never went back.

She felt haunted by shadows. Desperate for spiritual guidance, she hesitated over the phone receiver. The last time she called her madrina, an automated message said the number was no longer in service. What did she expect? She was cut off. Her *Egun* and the *orishas* had nudged her long enough. Her godparents had washed their hands of her. She needed direction, someone to counsel her, but until she submitted to the *Asiento* ceremony, neither godparent would waste time on her. She had to surrender, to dedicate herself completely.

Before sunrise, Isabel woke covered in her own sweat. She ignited the gas range for eggs, and heard Esther's alarm clock beeping down the hall. She could hear the girl running water in the bathroom. She desperately wanted to know her daughter, to have the kind of intimate relationship she had always hoped for, but the girl had shut her out completely. Esther returned each day from school and withdrew into her bedroom. She even ate her meals alone on her bed, headphones muffling her ears. The girl walked shadowy in and out of the house, so quiet, so secretive. Isabel didn't trust her. An unguarded teenage girl was not safe in this world. She told Isabel nothing about her friends anymore, nothing about her life. What was she hiding?

Isabel sat on the couch with a plate of eggs on her lap, a cup of coffee on the side table, the morning news blasting from the television. She was sick of eating alone. The house felt oppressive and empty. She needed time to think. Now Esther was pushing her away, too. Something had to be wrong with her daughter. Why else would she have these dreams? She had no idea what had gotten into the girl, but things didn't add up. Isabel's mind spiraled with possibilities. Lourdes said the *orishas* were known to use brute force to get their way. What if they hurt Esther?

Each Monday, Isabel left a special offering at the foot of her *Egun* statue, something to protect her baby girl, something to bless their finances, to keep the family in good health. In her mind, she imagined the *Egun* say, *Too little, too late.*

No matter what she did, the nightmares persisted. In the morning, after Esther left for school with Tío Maximo, Isabel sat wracked with nervous energy. She set about to cleaning the house. Sometimes, she smoked on the front porch, watching the palm trees in the breeze or the occasional car rattle by. She missed her view of the sailboats crossing the Long Island Sound. Nothing stilled her shaking hands.

She needed to clear her head. She sat in a chair in front of the television the way her madrina had taught her back in New York. She set the television on a blurry station of gray lines and muted the volume. Isabel breathed deeply.

She sat on the couch and stared at the blurred lines bouncing on the television screen. With her mind, she reached out, her inner gaze fixated on the static and the chaos. If something dangerous was in the air, if something was coming, she felt determined to know it, to stop it. She reached her mind outward, her consciousness extending toward the television. Her madrina said spiritual currents traveled through the screen. Electrified, she transferred her consciousness into the energy body of the television to see reality through fresh eyes.

Her madrina told stories of using this method to leave her own body and walk around her Bronx neighborhood, but Isabel didn't like to venture far. She never left the house. It was enough to simply slip into the television. From the screen, she looked back and could see her own limp body reclining on the couch, a silver umbilical cord linking her body with her projected spirit.

From this perspective, she could see how thin she had become, how old, how transformed. Her hair grayed at the roots, her red nail polish chipped at the ends. Frown lines creased the corners of her mouth. She didn't like to see herself this way, fraying at the edges. She shifted her attention to the rooms beyond the rooms, longing to speak with her *orishas*, but they hid. She had disobeyed, delayed the *Asiento* ceremony, and now they all withdrew their protection from her.

Meditation didn't help. She couldn't plug the stream of doubts and anxious thoughts running through her mind. Her prayers and offerings made no difference. Isabel felt desperate. Even in a trance, she couldn't shake her feeling of dread. She forced herself to awareness and walked into Esther's bedroom. She sifted through the desk drawer, noticed the books beside the neatly made daybed. She scanned the bookshelves, the cassette tapes, examined the clothes in the closet. Everything was in its place. Isabel opened the underwear drawer and reached her hand beyond the cotton panties. From the very back, she pulled out Esther's private diary and began to read where she had left off the day before.

THE LAMB

Puerto Rico
1950

Paula heard the bark of the neighbor's dog before she noticed the car approaching. She rose from the kitchen table in her nightgown and cracked the shutters. Outside, the broken pavement sloped precariously toward the plaza. In the opposite direction, wooden shacks lined the road until it dead-ended at a narrow strip of beach where pigs grazed on garbage. Anxious for Rosendo to come home, she watched the headlights creep closer. She pulled on her cotton robe and stepped outside.

The day's news had suffocated her small house with revolution. Neighbors had stopped in and out with fresh rumors, wringing their hands over the bombings and bemoaning the five Nationalists riddled with bullets on the steps of the governor's palace.

After dark, she had turned off the radio and ordered the children to bed despite their protests. Enough, she had told them. She held a leather belt and wasn't afraid to use it. Her head pounded. In two hours, the baby would need another feeding. Just a few hours of silence, no more words, please. Her body ached.

If she had been more like Rosendo, she would have grabbed the *pitorro*, a raw rum they kept stashed in the cabinet above the chamber pot, something to numb the blood and thicken the walls. But she never drank. She never played the numbers, never played cards, and she certainly never danced the *bomba*. At carnival time, while Rosendo raised hell in the village and pawed girls half her age, she confined herself to her home as if she were taking shelter

169

from a deadly storm. She washed and ironed clothes, mopped floors, and fried meats; in this way, she warded off a thousand devils, her mind humming, anticipating in advance the slightest thing that might upset him.

"I don't want none of you kids awake when your papi gets home." She would beat sleep into them if she had to. The three older girls squeezed onto a secondhand, queen-size bed, and the younger boys sullenly crowded onto cots. She made a furious threat when Joseph complained about one of the twins peeing the bed, but after that, the children settled, and she relaxed into the heavy breathing sounds of their fitful dreams.

She had just finished nursing Isabel when she heard the car. She placed the sleeping baby in the bassinet, suspecting the car was a *público* taxi driving Rosendo home.

She stood on the uneven front steps and watched the car creep closer. The night breeze rustled dry palms, and there were the sounds of *coquí* frogs and gravel crunching under tires. In the sharp beam of the headlights, she squinted and gripped the sagging door frame for support.

The engine silenced and the headlights went black, leaving only moonlight and the warm glow of a street lamp. For a few seconds, she went blind before her eyes adjusted. Most of the surrounding houses sat dark, but few houses were ever completely silent. From behind their wood walls and iron fences, she had grown accustomed to hearing dogs yelp, babies cry, couples quarrel, and the sound of a man doing his damage. There were no porch lights, but when a man stepped out of the black Plymouth, she recognized him almost immediately.

"Alberto, is Rosendo with you?" she said, keeping her voice to a whisper.

"No, I thought he was here with you."

She shook her head. "He left in a fit toward San Juan days ago."

"Oh, Christ! Why? He isn't involved."

"Why do you think? To find you." She stood several feet away from the car, but she could feel the heat radiating off the metal.

He stepped closer to the house. From her elevated position on the front steps she could make out the shadowy details of his face. "You look exhausted," she said.

"You, too."

"I couldn't sleep. I saw the car lights and thought you were a taxi."

"Or maybe the insular police?" He laughed uneasily.

"That's not funny."

"How long has he been gone?"

"Two days. He's taken off before, but he always comes home. A neighbor has a telephone. I thought maybe I should call the hospital."

"Wouldn't make a difference," he said. "The phone lines have been cut."

Her eyes widened. "Cut? The whole city?"

"The whole island," he said.

She pictured the island of Puerto Rico set adrift, cut loose from the rest of the world and floating. "Who would do that?"

"Maybe the Nationalists, maybe the Yankees? Who knows? Either way, no news is getting on or off the island tonight." She heard the disappointment in his voice. "They plan to crush us," he said.

In her heart, she had never held out for independence. Maybe once it could have worked, but not anymore. When Puerto Ricans were finally permitted to vote for their own governor in 1948, she had cast her ballot for the more moderate Luis Muñoz Marín. His campaign of *Pan, Tierra, Libertad* had made sense to her. That was, of course, before the gag laws, before the *carpetas*, before the martial law rulings, and before the use of the National Guard. She would take her vote back, if she could. Still, in the newspapers, Governor Muñoz Marín had claimed that the Nationalists were working with the Reds.

She studied Alberto's face. Maybe Rosendo was right. Maybe Alberto had chased after shifting-sand dreams.

"So, what now?" she said. "You've been gone for weeks."

171

"I know."

"And before that, I waited thirteen years."

"I tried to come back sooner," he said. "You do believe me, don't you?" He removed his hat and fidgeted with the brim. She sensed his brokenness, but she couldn't help feeling angry. She was a mother, and he had no right. And worse, despite all the years of disappointment, she still loved him, perhaps would always love him, and he still chose the island over her. He'd made her wait for him, not once, but twice. How could she be so stupid?

"You said two weeks," she bit out.

"The roads around the capital are all blocked. They're arresting everyone. I got back as soon as I could."

"Not soon enough."

He looked down at his feet, and when he spoke, she could barely hear his words. "You have no idea." He appeared to be speaking to himself, an ironic smile twisting the corners of his mouth. He stepped toward her, slowly, and she thought for a second he might grab her, kiss her right there in front of the small house where her children slept. Her eyes widened with desire as she pressed her back against the door. Perfectly trapped. When he didn't kiss her, but instead sat on the steps at her slippered feet, she felt like a fool. Of course. He isn't here for you, she told herself. She was no longer a *señorita*, maybe she never was. *Old soul*, her brother had called her. Now she just felt plain old.

She looked down at his slender shoulders and jet hair, and tried to think of something reasonable to say. "I'm worried about Rosendo." She adjusted her robe over her bare knees. "I'm tempted to go find him and drag him back here myself."

"He should have waited at the house, like I said."

"Since when does the man listen? He couldn't wait. He was going stir crazy cooped up in this house. For days, on the radio, there's been nothing but talk of revolution. Then we heard how they shot up that man you were looking for."

"You mean Vidal?"

"The whole shoot-out was aired live on the radio."

"I know," he said. "People watched for hours, cheering him from the streets."

"The radio man on WMDD said the *salón* had thirty Nationalists inside. We thought you might be there." She had to catch her breath before she spoke again. "It's all so awful, and the kids were asking questions, but I didn't know what to tell them. After that, it all just got worse. It's like I blinked, and the whole world changed overnight."

"Nothing's changed," he said. "Nothing ever changes."

"I've changed." She lowered her eyes.

He studied her face. "Not a chance. You look exactly the way I remember."

She blushed, embarrassed.

"I was never in the barber's building," he said. He lifted his gaze to her. "Knowing you, you said a lot prayers for nothing." A wry smile crossed between them. "Wasted breath," he said.

"Not wasted," she said. "You're here, that's all that matters. What happened?"

He flexed his fingers. "The radio stations had it all wrong. It's true, Vidal was my contact in Santurce, but I know for a fact that he held off the police *and* the National Guards all alone. I never stepped foot in the building. So you see, you worried for nothing."

"Not for nothing. The radio said there were thirty men at least—"

"I don't care what the radio said. I saw it. I watched the whole thing. I couldn't stop it, nobody could. The police blocked the road, and all I could do was duck for cover and watch." Alberto pressed his thumb and middle finger against his eyes and inhaled, making circular motions with the tips of his fingers. She noticed his hand trembling, but said nothing.

When he opened his eyes again, he looked up at the half moon as if ready to howl. "Soldiers and snipers surrounded the salón Baricua with machine guns and even a bazooka," he said. "They shot the place to hell."

"How awful!"

"I'm not what you think, Paula. I wish . . ." He pushed hair out of his eyes. "I hid like a child when they attacked Vidal. Like a coward." He stared at the ground, and the hair slipped over his eyes once again.

"You couldn't stop what happened."

"He shouldn't have been alone."

She paused, cleared her throat. "I don't understand. Why so much fighting over one man?"

"They didn't know he was one man, didn't know he was alone. For three hours, he held them off with everything he had— Molotov cocktails, submachine guns. The works."

"Why would one barber have all those weapons? It makes no sense."

"Remember, I told you. He was the barber of Pedro Albizu Campos. Nationalists had been hiding weapons in the salón Baricua for years."

From a neighboring second-floor balcony, they heard the strike of a match and saw the red tip of a cigarette flame in the dark.

"Do you want to come inside?" she asked. She imagined him sitting at her table while she heated coffee on the charcoal stove. Mentally, she scanned her kitchen shelves and wondered if the smell of fried green bananas would wake the children.

He looked over his shoulder toward the balcony and narrowed his eyes. She followed his gaze. Perhaps more curious neighbors sat on invisible shabby porches in flimsy rocking chairs.

"I shouldn't stay long," he said. "I came to get what's mine and go."

"And then what?"

"Stay out of sight. All the leaders are either dead, arrested, or on the run." He shrugged. "It's just a matter of time before some hooligan rats me out."

"Then stay here," she said, almost pleading. "Just a little while, until things on the street settle down."

He sounded angry. "You mean hide? Just crawl into a hole in the earth and hide. Is that the idea?"

"Why not? You hid when they attacked Vidal, didn't you?"

His head snapped up.

"I'm sorry. That was unfair," she said. "He was your friend."

"I'm no fugitive," he said softly. "But I won't ever go back to the cooler. I'd rather die than go back to jail."

She threw up her hands. "God, why won't you leave while you still can? And I don't just mean San Juan. While you have air in your lungs and half a brain in your head, go to Nueva York and make a life."

"That's just it. It doesn't matter where I go. There is no life without freedom. I get it now. Revolutionaries give all that up, that's what they do. They die."

"So, you want to end up like the others, riddled in bullets?" She felt her voice growing louder in anger. "Is that what you're saying? There's no other way?"

"Independence is the only way."

"You said it yourself. Independence is crushed. The sooner you accept that, the better."

"I said no such thing."

She had to convince him somehow. "Don't you think you could make more of a difference for this country if you live? Live by the sword, die by the sword. You know I'm right. Every breath is a gift from God, and you're gonna throw all that away."

"Always preaching," he said with a sad smile.

She was furious at him, yet at the same time it felt good to talk in the familiar way she'd almost forgotten she could. "Men and women, we just see the world differently, that's all," she said, "All this violence will only set us back. It'll end in more violence."

"You're pretty smart, you know that."

"For a woman? Is that what you mean?"

He shook his head. "Albizu Campos says women are the expression of the nation, the highest expression of our race."

Paula shrugged. "I don't know. I've never seen women like that around here." She sighed deeply. "All I see is women getting slapped around, chased with sticks, kicked when they're down.

Don't matter what the flag looks like. They slip under a man and disappear."

"You're still here," he said, squeezing her arm.

"I'm a ghost. Not half the woman I used to be."

"I don't believe that for a second. You're raising eight beautiful children. Looks to me like you're tough as nails, the general of a small army."

"Just promise me, you'll leave. Get out of here and live. There's no greater resistance than that. Your life *is* resistance."

With his hand still on her arm, he gave her a piercing look. "You could come with me."

She froze. "Don't," she said, pushing his hand off her. "I'm a mother."

"You don't have to tell me who you are," he said. "I know exactly who you are. I've always known you. You know me, too." He cupped her face in his hands and leaned toward her, spoke so closely that she could feel his warm breath on her skin. "Come with me."

"Stop saying that."

"I hear what you're saying. And maybe you're right. In Nueva York the independence movement has growing support. The Nationalists have a strong network there, and I could . . . we could . . ."

"There is no *we*, Alberto."

He removed his hands from her face. "Even when you ran off with Rosendo, I never blamed you. I blamed only myself. For all of it."

"I didn't run off with him. Not like that. Anyway, it was a long time ago. None of that matters now. Look, I've changed my mind," she said, standing to her feet. "I think you should get what you came for and leave."

He had an arch tilt in his jaw. "What if it's you I came for? What then?"

"You don't know what you're saying. You have no idea what you're asking me to do."

"I'm sorry. I've made you uncomfortable."

"The crates buried under my house, that's what makes me uncomfortable. I can hardly sleep knowing any minute the police could storm in here."

"I wouldn't let that happen."

"As if you could change a single hair on your head. Just go." She felt exhausted, unhinged. "Get out of here before Rosendo comes back. Sell what you can, make a new start in the States."

"It's too risky. Even if I wanted to, I can't sell what's in the crates right now," he said. "The island is swarming with the National Guard. My instructions were to deliver the crates to Vidal and him alone. Now that he's gone, it's complicated."

She felt sick to her stomach. "But the boxes can't stay here."

"I promise you, no one knows. That's why I came to you in the first place. You're not involved. I need to wait till things die down, but as soon as I can, I'll unload the crates and use the money to leave for good, just like you said. But I'm serious. I want you to come with me."

"I told you, I can't."

"Not just you, then. Rosendo, too. And in time, we'll send for the whole family."

"All of us?"

"Yes. If that's what it takes."

"I won't abandon them."

For a long time, neither one spoke. They stared across the lane at the dark, unpainted shacks with their gabled rooftops. On the breeze, she smelled a hint of cigarette smoke.

"Let's go inside," she said.

"What about your children? Aren't they sleeping?"

"It's fine. We'll be quiet."

"And your neighbors?" He shot a quick glance out of the corner of his eye toward the cigarette smoke.

"Ay, let them gossip. I'm too old for sweethearts."

He followed her inside, swatting a moth and several mosquitoes away from the open door as they flew toward the light.

She peeked behind the curtain into the dark bedroom where her children slept. When she looked back, she noticed Alberto moving a basket of clothes from a kitchen chair and placing it on the cement floor before sitting down at the table.

She normally kept an immaculate house, but now she looked around the room and noticed the misplaced mop and the shabby table. She had been distracted all day by the news, the neighbors coming in and out, the children.

He placed his hat on the table as she poured water from a jug into the kettle.

"I know people in Nueva York. They could help us find an apartment, work." He seemed energized, illuminated by the idea.

"Where would we live? This is our home." She didn't mention that she and Rosendo lived on a small plot of land given to them by Governor Muñoz Marín, who during the elections had given plots of land in exchange for votes.

"Listen," he said. "I need to tell you something."

She didn't look at him. Instead, she brushed away some old ash and picked up a few cinders to reuse.

"I'm married. Her name is Elena."

She felt foolish. Of course he had a woman. Thirteen years had passed between them. "Good," Paula said flatly. "I'm glad you're not alone."

"It wasn't a good match." He sighed and rubbed his fingers around the brim of his hat. "We married by justice of the peace ten years ago after the birth of our son, Felix, but the boy and Elena live with her mamá in Río Grande. It was no good from the start. We were young. But it doesn't matter. I can't abandon her here with the boy."

"Of course not. You'll do what's right, Alberto. I've always known that about you."

He laughed bitterly. "You see what you want to see in people. You've always been like that."

"I've grown up since then." She crumbled a sheet of newspaper and placed it on the grates of the stove.

"I can get four airplane tickets, Paula. Did you hear me? Four."

She placed the kettle on the grates, and when she turned to face him, she had tears in her eyes. "Who would take care of my children? I'm still nursing the baby at night." With trembling hands, she struck a match and held the flame to the newspaper to ignite the coal.

"I know it's a sacrifice, but it's not forever. Two couples can save twice as fast. If we share an apartment, share expenses, we'll have the money to send for Felix and your children in no time. You'll see."

She gaped at this. "Are you saying you think Rosendo and I should live with you and Elena? Is that what you're really saying? This is madness!"

Paula tried to imagine New York. Those she knew who had returned to the island from the city said it was plain rotten. They spoke of bitter cold, prejudice, and a concrete world without stars. Others returned after working one year in the States with enough money to buy a house.

Determined, Alberto said, "Your oldest, Juanita, isn't she old enough to watch the baby? Wouldn't your family in Fajardo take the kids, just for a while, just until we can send for them?"

"Yes," she allowed, "but the twins are only four, and the other girls are in school. Who would keep them out of trouble? When Angelito isn't at school, he sells fruit on the side of the road, but it isn't nearly enough." She tried to imagine her children without her, but the idea felt unbearable.

"What isn't enough?" a voice boomed from the porch.

Rosendo walked through the door as though he hadn't been gone for three days without explanation. His eyelids were so heavy that he stumbled and braced himself with the back of a chair. He reeked of rum, cigars, and days-old sweat. He glared at Alberto and then at Paula, who would not meet his eyes. "What the hell? You're a hard man to find, and here I find you at my own goddamn table."

Alberto rose slowly from the chair. "I came to see you. Where have you been?"

"Where have *I* been?" Rosendo slumped into a chair and kicked off his shoes and socks. The soles of his feet were dry, bark-like, his nails yellowed and thick. "*Cabrón*, where have *you* been?"

179

Alberto slowly sat, not taking his eyes off his brother.

"Some big shot you are," said Rosendo. "I asked around at the docks. No one's even heard of you." He looked disdainful. "When that turned out to be a dead end, I ended up playing bingo and shooting craps with my *compadres*."

"For three days?" said Alberto sarcastically.

Paula imagined a fair-skinned woman, slimmer, younger. She knew Rosendo took up with other women when he went to Viejo San Juan. She smelled their flowery perfume on his clothes, saw the love bites on his neck. Still, she bit her own tongue and said nothing.

"Don't give me that dirty look," he said, shooting a sharp glance at Paula.

She turned to the stove to remove the boiling kettle with an oven mitt.

"Look, forget it," said Alberto. He leaned forward and spoke quickly. "We have things to settle, plans to make. I've been thinking—"

Paula heard a whimper from the bedroom, and used it as an excuse to leave the room. "The baby has a bad rash," she said under her breath, but neither man seemed to hear. She pulled the curtain aside and slipped into the bedroom, navigating the dark room like a nocturnal cat. She lifted the baby from her bassinet, and for a moment, she stood in the dark, holding the girl close to her chest, breathing her in.

"Mami," said Angel. "Is Papi home?"

His voice startled her. "Yes, go back to sleep."

"Is he in bad shape?"

"What kind of question is that?"

"You know what I mean."

"Keep out of it, *mijo*. I'm fine."

She felt like she was failing him. She could no more protect him than she could herself, and when he looked at her lately, she saw resentment mixed with pity. He skipped school regularly, but she didn't dare tell Rosendo, afraid of the unbridled fury he would unleash on the boy. Paula felt the urge to lie down beside her children, but heard the men muttering in the other room. She couldn't leave them alone together for too long. She needed time to think. A moment to herself. What did she want? She teetered in limbo, so much like her beloved *país*, unsure of herself, unsure of everything.

"Never mind about your papi. I'll take care of him," she said. "Get some rest, and no matter what you hear, don't you leave this room. Understand?"

By the time she sat back at the table, she heard Alberto coaxing Rosendo, trying to convince him, but Rosendo's guarded expression revealed only distrust.

"Under the same roof?" he was saying. "You've got to be kidding."

Alberto smiled. "To get ahead, you need to take risks. You're a gambling man."

"It's too soon," Paula said. "Maybe when the baby's older, we could—"

"Nobody asked you," he growled. "If I want your opinion, I'll ask for it."

"Look, it's late," said Alberto. "All I ask is that you think it over. My wife, Elena, has an uncle who has been trying to get us to the States for years. He says there are many there who are sympathetic to our cause. He'll put me up in the city until I can get settled. Once I get an apartment and a job, I'll send for you and Elena. Think of how quickly we could save if we worked together, shared the expenses. It's the only way to make the money stretch. Look around. This world is falling apart."

Rosendo nodded. "You're serious?"

Alberto met Paula's concerned gaze. "We'll pave the way for the children. I swear it."

MAKING THE SAINT

Cuba
1989

The moment their Cuban Air flight touched down in Havana, the passengers onboard clapped with enthusiasm. Isabel's skin prickled. Dread crept into the pitiful corners of her mind, and her *Egun* berated her in her imagination. *This is your last chance.*

Ruben, one of Ernesto's godsons, a distinguished man who looked to be in his mid-fifties, welcomed Ernesto and Lourdes with warm enthusiasm. When he kissed Isabel's cheek and smiled, she saw he had several gold teeth and knowing eyes. Her skin felt paper thin, transparent, her face readable, her smile forced. Could he see that she was a fraud?

Under the surface of her decision to make saint was the relentless shame of feeling unlovable. No prescriptive spell had inched her closer to knowing her true self, and as she hid that shameful secret, she felt like an imposter. Inside, the fear of being revealed as a hack made her want to vomit. She didn't consciously acknowledge these feelings. When she arrived in Cuba, she couldn't articulate why her stomach balled into a fist or why her legs trembled. All she knew was she felt all wrong in the marrow of her bones.

Ruben helped Isabel and Lourdes with their luggage and escorted them to his car, an aquamarine 1956 Cadillac.

"Nice car," said Ernesto. "An antique."

"The engine is a Peugeot, diesel," said Ruben, his expression a mix of pride and good humor. "The rest is duct tape."

Isabel could see the roads were peppered with 1950s sedans and Russian Ladas, a time warp of classic cars. In the town center, a taxi line looked like cars parked outside a sock hop: a 1955 Chevrolet Bel Air, a 1957 Ford Fairlane with bright red interior, a 1955 Pontiac. Jude would have gotten a kick out of these cars, and she imagined how he and Ruben would have talked engines for days. She found it strange to think of Jude, here in Havana, years after their divorce, but stepping into Havana was like opening a time capsule. Jude, also a relic of the fifties, would have fit right in.

Regret frayed at the hem of her thoughts. Her need for control drove him away, and in the end, blaming him for abandoning her came easier than facing the truth.

As they drove, she noticed smoke billowing out of exhaust pipes, the roosters on rooftops, and the colonial-style buildings with their chipping paint. Sedans, mopeds, horses, bicycle taxis, and pedestrians shared the streets with the unhurried pace of a bygone era. The further they drove, the more she realized there was no going back.

When Isabel had agreed to book their flights out of Tijuana to Havana, she hadn't realized the capital city would be both beautifully seductive and disenchanting all at once. The colonial buildings, with their balconies, rounded archways, and columns, teetered between ruin and romantic charm. Here were a people disillusioned by the promises of a demigod, a tyrant. Somehow it felt deeply personal. A thousand tiny degradations had brought her to this crossroad, and not for the first time, she wondered if she should jump out of the car and run.

When Isabel asked about the peeling paint and collapsing buildings, Ruben explained that many of the restoration projects had been put on hold. There were rumors that Soviet troops would be withdrawing from Cuba soon as ties between Castro and the Kremlin crumbled. "We've tightened our belts," said Ruben. "Rations on food and gas are strict."

With one hand, Isabel adjusted the elastic money belt under her blouse for the third time. In Mexico, she had exchanged seven thousand dollars into Mexican pesos, and the stuffed belt cinched tightly around her waist. Her skin felt moist and hot beneath the coarse nylon.

In Old Havana, they stood in line outside a bank for thirty minutes to exchange Mexican pesos for Cuban pesos. Confused, Isabel said to Ruben, "Are you sure it's open?" Sweat dripped down the back of her shirt. She looked inside where two clerks stood in the dark, looking bored and preoccupied in quiet conversation with one another, ignoring the line. "All the lights are off," she said.

"Electricity shortage," Ruben said. He glanced inside, nodded and smiled. "After baseball, standing in line is our national sport. Don't worry, you'll get used to it."

Shopping for Isabel's *Asiento* ceremony was more complicated than she'd expected. Because of the rations and because of what Ruben referred to as "the special period," it took the rest of the day to find the herbs, oils, flowers, and meats. Ruben navigated Ernesto, Lourdes, and Isabel through one ramshackle apartment after another. In buildings with exposed wires and collapsing stairwells, they knocked on doors to purchase the fresh foods they couldn't find in the empty stalls on the street. Behind curtains, in cardboard boxes, and from under seat cushions, men and women flashed their black market goods—everything from stuffed sausage to feed the guests over the course of the week, to the ceremonial items such as coconut, pepper, sunflower and poplar leaves, bananas, and guava. Isabel had the feeling everything she purchased that day had fallen off the back of a truck, and she began to realize just how much she took for granted back home.

"People sell on the sly," said Ruben. "It's how we survive." He shrugged in resignation, but there was no bitterness in his words.

"Do you think about leaving?" she asked quietly. She imagined him floating away on a makeshift raft of car tires.

"Never," said Ruben. "This is my home." There was pride in his voice when he spoke. Maybe something else, too—condescension? Pity? She wondered how he could pity her when she lived freely. But did she? Could he sense that she felt like a puppet? Spiritually codependent on forces she did not love and did not trust.

All day, Ruben negotiated for the necessary items needed for her ceremony, and because people were suspicious of strangers and afraid of trouble with the authorities, he suggested he handle the money. Unsure whether or not she could trust him fully, Isabel looked nervously at Ernesto, who nodded in assurance. "I'm godfather to both Ruben and his brother," said Ernesto. "It's safer this way."

Isabel handed Ruben three hundred of the Cuban pesos she had exchanged at the bank. "Is this enough?"

The money was over a year's salary in Cuba, but she knew the week-long ceremony wouldn't be cheap. It would require she pay for the travel expenses, purchase the tools, vessels, herbs, animals, special clothing, meals for all the guests, and provide the stipend for each of her two godparents.

"This will work, for starters," he said. He took the wad of money, and without counting, shoved the bills into his pockets. Perhaps to reassure her, he told her that he had been a professor for a decade, but was accused of being anti-Communist and had lost his job. Now he made money as a religious tour guide, navigating visitors from all around the world who came to Cuba for authentic Santeria ceremonies.

"*No te preocupes*," Lourdes said. "Remember, not all godchildren become saints. Especially not in Cuba!" She squeezed Isabel's shoulder and smiled. "This was a calling, a right of passage reserved only for a few. You should feel grateful, mija."

"You're blessed," Ernesto added.

Isabel knew the *Asiento* had to be prescribed by the *orishas* themselves, approved by her *Egun* ancestors. She knew she should be thankful, but she wasn't. She felt backed into a corner. She convinced herself it was the only way to save Esther, who she suspected was out of control, hiding secrets, and perhaps in danger. Her daughter was possibly on an arc toward screwing up her whole future, and without the help of her *orishas*, how could she stop any of it?

*

They took a ferry over the harbor to the quiet town of Regla, where they rode a bicycle taxi down a main street called Martí. Here, there were fewer cars and squat cement houses that reminded Isabel of poor barrios in Puerto Rico. People walked up and down Calle Martí, chatting in dilapidated wooden doorways and sat in the plaza beside a dry fountain. On the curbs, men huddled over the hoods of classic cars, tinkering with corroded engines in order to raise them from the dead. All around were the sounds of men shouting to one another, babies crying, the voices of women, and blaring music from open windows. Everywhere she looked, she saw both decay and resilience, ingenuity and the sheer will to survive.

Ruben's brother Bernardo lived with his wife and four children on a narrow street lined with block houses in various degrees of deterioration. Lourdes wrapped an arm around Isabel's shoulder and said, "Here is where you'll be making saint."

Isabel forced a smile. "Great," she said. Her cheerful tone was unconvincing.

Lourdes told her to imagine a birthday party and a wedding combined. "It will be even better than you can imagine."

Doubt rose up in Isabel. The *Asiento* ceremony would require that she wear white for an entire year. More than that, she would also have to shave her head completely bald. She twirled a strand of her hair, now dyed acorn brown, around her pointer finger. She dreaded the idea of shaving her hair. How could she explain going away for an entire week and returning with a bald head? She chewed the inside of her cheek. Chemotherapy seemed like the only logical explanation. She'd tell Esther and her family she had cancer. Inside her suitcase, along with the all white skirts and blouses, she had packed a dark brown, chin-length wig. But what would her friends say when she refused to hug them or shake hands? How could she avoid pictures with her daughter all year long? And depending on which *orisha* crowned her in the end, there would be new rules, too, taboos, which she would have to write in her *libreta* and commit to memory, obey down to every detail.

One year seemed like a lifetime. Paula would never buy it. She'd take one look at the white clothes and the bald head and see right through the lie. She would never allow Isabel to step foot inside her house. She would cut her off completely.

After sunset, Ernesto, Lourdes, Ruben, and Isabel returned to the pier and descended to the banks. A light wind blew, and Isabel smelled the foul water of Havana Bay. She stood knee deep in the waters, trying not to think of raw sewage, and waited for Lourdes to cut her clothes to shreds. Isabel, the *iyawo*, would be like a baby, and Lourdes would play the role of caring for her in every way, bathing her, feeding her, even escorting her to the bathroom. As Lourdes acted out the maternal role of godmother, Isabel sensed each step marching her toward a precipice.

With sharp scissors, Lourdes made the first cut and used her strong hands to rip the fabric apart. Isabel covered her chest with one arm and Lourdes blocked her naked body from the shore, where Isabel feared being noticed. Then Lourdes took a bar of soap and rubbed it on Isabel's skin in circular motions. Isabel felt the oily water and soap mix on her body and wished Lourdes would move faster. She felt exposed. Ernesto and Ruben stood guard, their backs to the women, their eyes locked on the flickering gas lights illuminating the street above.

Lourdes held a white towel over her left shoulder, and when she was finished with the bathing ritual, she wrapped the towel around Isabel and led her back on the shore. That night, Isabel slept at Bernardo's home on a grass mat, and in the morning, Lourdes repeated the bathing routine, but thankfully, this time, in the bathtub with herbs.

Lourdes dressed her in blue gingham and told her to meditate and remain on the mat beside the front door. She was not permitted to speak apart from proper greetings. "Remember, you are a baby," she said. That day, people dressed in all white entered the house to participate in the festivities, and several women busied themselves in the kitchen preparing meals for the guests using the meats and ingredients Isabel had purchased the day before in Havana. The small house filled quickly with people and the delicious smells of roasted meats and fried plantains. Lourdes instructed Isabel to remain at the door and greet each person who entered with the appropriate greeting. To show respect, each *orisha* had a particular type of greeting. When a priest of Eleguá arrived, she positioned her body facedown on the ground, then propped herself up on one side with an elbow, and then repeated on the other side. Then the elder helped her to her feet, crossed his arms over his chest, and gave her his blessing.

Lourdes warned her to get rest between each new guest's arrival. "You'll be up and down half the day," she said.

Ruben pulled up in front of the house. Rather than walk through the living room, he and his brother carried several large boxes onto the patio. Isabel knew the boxes held four-legged animals and birds for sacrifice, but she wasn't sure which ones. Ruben had assured her he would check each animal, taking great care to choose only the healthiest and fattest. Even with meat so scarce, there would be ritual sacrifice. Without it, nothing could be done. It was humbling to see everyone from Ruben's *casa de santos* working tirelessly on her behalf. She felt guilty about her doubts and anxious, watching the frenzy around her, dreading each next step.

Lourdes dressed Isabel in a royal blue gown, the colors of Yemayá. They had purchased the beautiful dress in Old Havana along with a teardrop fan, ornamental belt, the red, parrot-feathered crown, and the satin fabrics for the canopy throne.

Inside the dismal living room, furniture had been moved to make space for a large canopy draped with royal blue satin, white, red, and metallic cloth. Isabel felt a lump rise in her throat. The throne was magnificent. She had seen initiates with their shaved heads in years past standing under similar canopies dressed in similar eighteenth-century clothes.

Lourdes said she looked like an African princess. She guided Isabel to sit on a *pilón*, where each of the elders would take part in shaving her head under the canopy throne. From the patio, Isabel heard the bleating sound of sheep and goats whose throats would soon be sliced. She saw Lourdes approaching, hair clippers in hand,

and imagined the clumps of her hair falling to the ground, imagined the warm blood wiped over her head, chest, and legs, imagined, the *bata bata* of the drums, the trance, and the procession, and wanted to make it all stop. Terror welled up inside her.

She stood from the *pilón* and held out one shaky arm to steady herself. "Can we just . . . Can we wait a second?" She felt like she might vomit. "I need a second."

"Sit down," Lourdes commanded not unkindly.

Isabel's vision blurred.

In a sympathetic tone, Lourdes said, "It's normal to feel nervous."

She took a step back, bumping into the satin fabric of the throne. The elders circled around her, looking concerned and a little shocked.

Ernesto approached and spoke with a tinny voice. "What are you doing, mija?"

"I don't know." Isabel's eyes darted around the room, a maze of people. "I don't know anymore." Agitated, she said, "I thought I knew, but . . . I don't. You told me to trust my Ori, but there are so many voices in my head, I no longer know which is mine."

"This is just the beginning," he said. "Baby steps." He touched the top of her head to bless her. "After you are crowned here with your *orishas*, you'll never be alone. My saints are always with me. Where I go, they go. You'll see. It'll be the same with you."

His words, intended to comfort, simply left her with a tense knot in her stomach.

"That's the thing," she said, stepping away from his touch. "That might be all right for you, but it's not for me." Saying the words aloud solidified them in her mind. Here she was, surrounded by her elders, supposedly taking a leap of faith, but she felt like she was being shoved over a cliff face.

"Maybe you should sit down?" Ernesto said. Though he phrased it as a question, it was clearly a command.

Ernesto looked back at Lourdes. She could see from the confused expression on his face that no one had ever interrupted the *Asiento* ceremony before. Ernesto nodded to the back bedroom, and the elders cleared a narrow path for Isabel to walk through the living room and into one of the bedrooms.

Still dressed as Yemayá in her elaborate gown, she closed the door and sat on the bed. She felt ashamed and weak. Here she was repairing her broken relationship with her godparents, and now she was disappointing them all over again, and in front of the elders and other godchildren. In her mind, she heard the voice of her *Egun* demand she march right back under the canopy throne and finish what she'd started. Obey.

She squeezed her eyes and clenched her fists, willing the voices to silence. She had spent over a decade making venerations to her *Egun*, negotiating and tiptoeing around jealous spirits, demanding *orishas*. The *Asiento* would crown her with a new consciousness, a new being. She would have to leave in order for the *orisha* to enter. She would have to vanish. Could that really be her path, to surrender her own essence only to be displaced?

In Old Havana, she had seen a poster of a young Castro that read *Libertad o Muerte*, but when she looked around the city, she saw that there was not even the freedom to sell a single sausage. Here she was, offering more and more of herself, and if she continued, there would be nothing left to give. This was her last chance at freedom. Even if it meant a bolt of lightning striking her dead, she needed to leave, and she needed to do it now.

In her purse, which sat on the dresser, she carried her passport, the remainder of her money, and her travel visa back to Tijuana. From there, she could buy tickets to Puerto Rico.

Her eyes darted from the purse to the open bedroom window. Unlike in Puerto Rico, the window in Bernardo's bedroom faced the street and was not locked by iron bars. She heard the murmur of voices in the living room, heard footsteps approaching in the hall.

Before it was too late, before she could change her mind, she grabbed her purse with the money belt still inside, flung back the sheer bedroom curtains, and swung her leg over the ledge. She was half in and half out the window when Lourdes opened the door. A look of pure anguish streaked her face.

"What do you think you're doing?"

Isabel met her madrina's eyes. "I'm so sorry, but I can't," she said.

"Where is your *cara*, your courage?" There was a fire in Lourdes' voice now. "You're too impulsive, mija. Don't fall off your path when you've come so close. You're fighting me, fighting your ex, fighting the *orishas*. Don't you see? It's just a war with yourself."

"You've been good to me, *Madrina*. So good. You and Ernesto both. But I can't go through with this. I thought I could."

Lourdes warned her, saying she had to finish what she'd started. If she left now, they wouldn't be able to protect her. "It could mean tragedy, for you and your family. You know this." Her eyes filled with tears, her voice was pleading, and Isabel could see that she, too, was afraid.

"No more predictions," said Isabel. She was tired of people telling her the immeasurable horrors her future held. "I'll take my chances. It's my choice."

Then she ran. Barefoot, dressed in the satin gown of an eighteenth-century monarch, she ran down Bernardo's street, passing caved-in buildings and poor row houses. At the corner, thinking she was a vision, a woman pushing a stroller saw Yemayá, the maternal and fierce ruler of seas, running toward her, and crossed herself in the name of the *Padre, Hijo, y del Espiritu Santo*.

Isabel hailed a bicycle taxi, who peddled her through the narrow streets behind old cars spewing exhaust. She choked and covered her nose. On Calle Martí, a group of young boys kicking a deflated soccer ball pointed and waved at Yemayá on the bicycle. At the pier, waiting for the ferry, she offered a teenage girl five pesos to buy the cheap pair of flip-flops right off her feet. Hearing her accent, the girl realized she was a *yuma*, a foreigner, and the girl insisted on ten dollars in pesos in exchange for the shoes, half a month's wage.

Isabel returned on the ferry back to Old Havana, and when she arrived at the Habana Libre by taxi, she was drenched in sweat and covered in soot.

From the hotel lobby, she booked a room and purchased a sundress.

Standing on the balcony on the twenty-first floor, she looked out at the expanse of buildings below. The voices inside her head told her to jump. Loud, persistent voices emerged from the pit of her self-doubt. She wanted to live, more than ever before, not as a saint but as herself, which was somehow more sanctified than sainthood. Only she wasn't quite sure who she was anymore. The unknowable, unsayable parts of her being were a mystery to even herself. Even so, she stepped back from the balustrade. Evil omens or not, she had to make her own way. For the first time in her life, she trusted that life itself was the ultimate anointing.

RESISTANCE

New York
1950

Alberto found the Pitt Street tenement when he saw a *To Let* sign hanging from the iron fire escape, and he paid one month's rent in advance. Theirs was a dark, unventilated flat where, a hundred years earlier, European immigrants had squeezed in with rats the size of small dogs.

First, Alberto sent for Elena. Several weeks later, in the depths of winter, Paula and Rosendo arrived, each in haggard, plaid wool coats, one suitcase in hand and fifty dollars combined. It took Alberto over an hour to find them at the airport, and when he did, they looked confused and airsick. On the taxi ride, Paula squeezed between the brothers as Alberto told of the jobs he had arranged for them on assembly lines. He and Rosendo would work in a factory assembling wood furniture, while the women would work alternating shifts for Nestlé Chocolate.

The one-room apartment on Pitt Street had little furniture and felt as cold as an icebox.

"At least you don't have to sleep on the floor," Elena said by way of introduction.

Elena was entirely different than Paula had imagined. Tall and slender, she was an attractive woman with a kind, heart-shaped face, wispy, jet-black hair, and a full, pouty mouth. She talked incessantly, hardly coming up for air.

"We will sleep in the bedroom," Elena said. "There's only the one. It's the size of a chicken coop, but we manage. You and Rosendo will sleep here in the kitchen."

"It's not paradise," said Alberto, "but you'll be comfortable."

"We sleep with the lights on," Elena frowned. "To keep the rats away."

"The two bathrooms are in the hall," Alberto said. "We share with the flat next door, *Cubanos* from Havana."

"Alberto got you a cot," said Elena.

"We're very grateful," Paula said, and she meant it. She knew sharing their small apartment was a sacrifice, but for the sake of the children, the families would manage.

"Don't worry," said Alberto. "It's not as bad as it looks."

Paula and Elena took the bus that Monday morning, and Elena explained the route to the factory.

"The boss man will ask you one question only," said Elena. "Do you speak English? Just smile and say, yes. You'll be fine."

Paula felt uneasy, and Elena squeezed her hand. "At least we're together," she said. "Together, it's not so lonely."

It hurt more than she had imagined to have her children so far out of her reach, out from under her protection, and she did her best to push down the creeping fears that wanted to rise up and drown her. She channeled the fear and grief into work at the factory, taking on two shifts several nights a week to save faster. But when Rosendo started spending more and more of his evenings out in *el barrio*, she began to panic and suspect the worst. If she confronted him, he raged, once punching a hole into the wall.

The men worked nine-hour shifts, and came home covered in wood dust. They took turns bathing in the kitchen, and afterward, they turned the tub into a table by placing a wood board on top. There they ate rice and beans but little meat.

In Puerto Rico, Isabel celebrated her first birthday and took her first step. That same week in New York, Alberto had chastised Rosendo for gambling away the money he should have been saving for his children.

When an apartment opened up on the second floor, Alberto and Elena moved out. "It's for the best," Alberto said. "If we stay any longer under the same roof, we're bound to kill each other."

"Besides," Elena said, "Felix is coming." She smiled a huge, elated smile. Paula tried to appear happy for them both, but her face twisted into something forced and pained. Elena gave her arm a squeeze. "It won't be too long for you."

But both women knew it was a lie. On Friday nights, Rosendo dressed in his best clothes and big-shotted around the neighborhood until morning. Confident he'd hit it big, he spent his extra cash on boxing matches or playing the numbers, and when Paula started hiding the money, he put beer on credit.

When Felix arrived from Puerto Rico, Elena doted over her son, kissing his cheek every time she walked in or out of a room. She couldn't get enough of how he'd grown, how skinny he looked, how mature he seemed. But Elena's joy only exasperated Paula's despair. Then, on the heels of his arrival, on a sunny April morning, a telegram arrived from Puerto Rico with the news that little Esau had died of yellow fever.

Paula was devastated. She blamed herself for leaving the children in Puerto Rico, and blamed Rosendo for gambling away their money. Her agony made her all the more determined to save the airfare and save it quickly. By depositing five dollars in small increments, she paid down the fare for *la Eastern* with the travel agent. Fearful of losing her way in a fog of grief, she worked twice as hard. She refused to give Rosendo her paychecks, and she ate only Campbell's soup for months. It took one full year for her to save enough money, but when she did, she felt as if she'd gone toe to toe with Rosendo and won.

When it came time to register the children in public school, she searched her documents but had no copy of Joseph's birth certificate. Since Joseph and the twins were only one year apart, she enrolled Joseph using Esau's papers. At school and in the neighborhood, teachers and students came to know Joseph solely by Esau's name, and the name stuck; so much so, that he became Jacob's surrogate fraternal twin, replacing Esau in every way. Joseph adopted his new name and new identity like a birthright.

Years later, he enlisted in the army, went to Vietnam, got married, registered to vote, and signed Esau, his dead brother's name, on the birth certificates of his children. In Puerto Rico, it was as if they had buried Joseph in dust. In New York, a proxy Esau lived in his stead.

She felt as though she, too, was a counterfeit version of her former self. Moving to the States had changed her. Her long hours at work, Rosendo's explosive rage, and the allure of the streets whittled away at the family she'd been so determined to preserve. She felt the massiveness of city life creeping in like unknowable shadows, slipping under the door cracks, seeping into the crevices behind the cabinets.

A day didn't go by that she didn't miss Esau, miss home. She missed the smell of fruit in the air. The lush green of the rainforest and the palms, the crystal beaches, the sound of tropical birds, and the warm breeze on her skin, and the blue, blue skies over waterfalls and lagoons. She had wanted a new life for her children, for herself, too. Now that she had those things, she could think only of the life they'd left behind.

*

In 1969, the year The Young Lords took to the streets with their garbage initiative, the furniture factory where Rosendo and Alberto worked went up in flames. The police sergeant showed up at the hospital and recorded Rosendo's testimony. He said Alberto had tried to kill him. It started when the two brothers, men in their sixties by this time, tangled in the cafeteria, a fistfight of gladiator proportions.

According to Rosendo, Alberto picked a fight during a night shift. "He wanted to kill me," he told Paula. With a crushed back and third-degree burns on his arms, Rosendo described to the police how he and his brother had pushed each other, banging into table saws and tipping trays of tools. They punched, scratched, and tore at one another like scrapping dogs and had to be pulled apart by the other workers.

198

Rosendo couldn't say how the flash fire erupted. He guessed sawdust had been ignited by the welders, but who could know for sure? All he remembered was running, a chaotic mass exodus, before the spindle monster dropped from nowhere, crushing his spine. By the time the fire trucks arrived, Rosendo was severely injured and Alberto was dead. The coroner said Alberto had died of cardiac arrest brought on by smoke inhalation. Rosendo told Paula that he himself had died, too. He said he remembered seeing the light and the voices of his mother and other ancestors. This was the seventh sign all over again, and he was reborn. For him, it was the beginning of a new life. For Paula, it was the end of an old one.

WHERE THE MOON RAGES

Puerto Rico
1989

From the Tijuana airport, Esther's mother called to say, "Pack your bags, we're going home."

Esther didn't bother to ask why or what she meant by *home*. She had seen this day coming. Going home to New York was not the same thing as going back. Her parents' marriage was now gutted. Still, New York was the only home she had, and that was better than no home at all. How could she begin to unpack the lies? Dust off the old secrets, rearrange the old arguments? Her fears drew close and circled around, all eyes, closing in like black birds.

Three year earlier, her parents had sold the waterfront Rochelle Street house to the Reverend Sun Myung Moon, and angry neighbors on the island complained in bitter letters and in editorials to the local paper that he and his gnostic sex cult lived like slobs, packing the rooms to the brim with brainwashed, vacant-eyed Moonies. Reverend Sun Myung Moon, a child eater like El Cuco, married off young girls in mass weddings, cloistering them in compounds in Westchester and Korea. Three decades later, after the Reverend died at age ninety-two, Esther would read in the *New York Post* how his children inherited the multi-billion dollar real estate empire but not their father's messianic ideals. "Our role is more of the apostles," Moon's son said in the article. "We become the bridge between understanding what kind of lives our two parents have lived."

Like Moon's son, she, too, filled the gaps, the hollow spaces between her parents. Her memories were merely bridges of fiction, myths, and magic fed to her by her mother. Which of her mother's stories were real? Which imagined? She no longer knew the difference or cared. Like the Moonies, her family was not welcome back to City Island. All of their bridges were burned, along with every spell book, amulet, prayer bead, goblet, resin saint statue, and talisman.

"We can't leave a single door open," her mother said. "Burn everything. What we can't burn, we'll throw in the river." Esther couldn't help but think that her mother's expression was that of a person pressing a sharp blade to a vein.

Before their flight from San Juan to JFK, she and her mother searched their house in Fajardo, frantic to find every hidden fetish. They peeked under the beds, opened the closets, rifled through coat pockets, and slid their palms along the rafters, gathering over a decade of her mother's magic into pillowcases and boxes. Afterward, they drove to a secluded river called Charco Frio, and dumped the pillowcases and boxes. The contents formed a pile on the rocks. Esther poked it into a tight bundle with a stick.

Her mother said each object worked like an invitation, an open door for the *orishas* to come and go through as they pleased. She said getting rid of the objects closed the doors, but keeping them sealed forever might be impossible.

"Are you scared?" Esther tossed the stick she held into the river.

"I was becoming something else, someone else I didn't recognize," her mother said. "I couldn't do it. I was so close, but I couldn't go through with it. Maybe I should be scared. But I'm not. For the first time, I'm not."

Fear had driven her mother's every impulse, and Esther inherited the fear like an ancestral curse. In flip-flops and jeans, Esther squatted along the river and peered into the crystal-clear water. She looked over her shoulder toward the parking lot. By midday, the rocks would be covered with picnics and tourists. Now, at dawn, they appeared slick, glistening.

"To make saint is to seal the *orisha* inside, trap it in your own skull." Her mother's voice snagged in her throat. "Look, if something bad happens to me—"

"Don't say that," Esther begged. "I don't want to think about that."

"Okay." Her mother made clean-slate promises. "Whatever it takes," she said. "From now on, it's just you and me." To cover all of her bases, as instructed by Grandma Paula, she rebuked the *Egun* and each of the *orishas* in the name of Jesus.

Esther shrugged. "That's it?" She had anticipated an *Exorcist* moment, a lightning strike that never came. There was only the sound of running water.

Her mother poured lighter fluid over the small pile of books and talismans, the cotton pillowcase, and the shredded boxes. She balanced a cigarette between her lips, struck a match, and lit the tip before tossing the match onto the pile. With a breathy puff of wind, a flame took hold and consumed the objects until they were only black ash. What they couldn't burn, they tossed into the river or carried back home in pockets of memory.

For the rest of her life, her mother slept with headphones on, listening to a continuous loop of Southern gospel preaching to keep out the rum-thickened voices of her ancestors. She joined the local church, joined the Sunday choir, joined the women's prayer breakfast, and in a moment of conviction, embraced forgiveness and agreed to remarry Esther's father. "He's my cross," her mother had said, but Esther couldn't help noticing the singular pleasure she took in her despair, her martyrdom.

The wedding was a private ceremony, and her parents were surrounded by strangers. They headed south on her father's Harley, a holy pilgrimage to Daytona's Bike Week. With the wind in their faces, the vibration between their thighs, and the loud hum of the engine, they followed a pillar of smoke to a biker church and performed a do-over wedding. In jeans and leather, the pastor pronounced them husband and wife. "It takes all kinds," the pastor had said. "We welcome Suzukis, Yamahas, Harleys, and Hondas."

Like a slave master, fear had driven Esther toward unattainable perfection in much the same way it had driven her mother on the path of the saints. It took decades before Esther learned to sit face to face with her shadows and to see her fear for its true self—a bunch of airy nothings desperate for love. Discerning truth from her mother's smoke and mirrors became her life-long *odu*, her path.

Now Esther's dreams of torrential floods and falling stars have grown quiet, and her phantom ancestors are not the dragons she once feared. When her grandmother died, followed by her father, she venerated them in her stories, casting holy words on pages. Words are made flesh. They are the offerings and prayer beads around her neck. One by one they make her born again. She imagines when she is done with this life, forget-me-nots will tangle where hair should be and a Ceiba tree will sprout out of her chest. Somewhere between bone and memory, there will be a heavenly host of saints. She will ripple downstream in the wake of their stories and marvel at so much unimaginable beauty.

ACKNOWLEDGEMENTS

I couldn't have written this book without the endless, loving support of my husband, David, and without the love and light of my children, Isabella and Micah. You ground my life with meaning. I also wish to thank my mom for courageously entrusting me with her stories and for the faith she bestowed on me to share them with the world.

For editorial support, my wholehearted gratitude to the amazing Jeff Parker for his guidance as a writing mentor. Your help made this a better book. Also, enormous thanks to Stefan Kiesbye for your generous time and kindness. You encouraged me to write from the places that scare me and helped me navigate when I felt blinded by the dark. My sincere appreciation to Corinna Vallianatos for your keen insight. Your vision to focus on the mothers and daughters alone helped me narrow my lens. I wish to also thank Erica Dawson, Sandra Beasley, Jason Ockert, Jessica Anthony, and the incredible support I received from many other phenomenal writers in my MFA program at the University of Tampa. Including my encouraging cohort Amanda Phoenix Starling, Chelsea Catherine, and Ernie Reynolds. Because of your unbelievable friendship, I felt less alone in the process.

Thanks also to Jessica Hatch for your brilliant editing of early drafts.

My whole heart to Jennifer Mathews and Brett Kelly Goldberg for sharing the weight and gift of childhood memories and reminding me that memory is often unreliabile. To the Hutchings family, Abby Wooten, Annie Engelman, and Matt Martin for believing in me, and to Kenny Jensen for your enthusiasm and inspiration. Gratitude to Jeff Daniel Marion for teaching me to write by ear and for taking me under your compassionate wing.

To the indispensable reference I learned from, *War Against All Puerto Ricans: Revolution and Terror in America's Colony* by Nelson A. Denis. To Krystal Quiles for her beautiful cover design, and to my agent Charlotte Sheedy for her invigorating support.

I am also deeply appreciative of my editor James Brubaker and SEMO Press for championing my work, opening doors, and helping me bring this book into the world.

And to my grandmother Paula, my dad, and the many other ancestors on the other side who bravely and graciously paved the way.